KAALI

By

SITHY FAZIL

Copyright ©2017 SithyHedges

All rights reserved.

About the Author

I was born in 1954 in Sri Lanka and came to live and settle in England in 1962 at the age of eight and have lived in the UK ever since. I am semi-retired and live and work in Surrey in Social Services. I previously worked for many years in finance.

I have many interests which include travel, reading, cooking and people.

I prefer to use my maiden name, Fazil, as my surname has changed a couple of times. I married to become a Sadiq but was widowed after 23 years of marriage and three children. I remarried and my current surname is Hedges but am now divorced.

Kaali is my debut novel, loosely referencing to my life experiences in both continents and my journey to the United Kingdom by ship.

However, I assure everyone that this book is pure fiction and any events and likeness to characters is completely coincidental.

Note on Rewriting novel.

About the Book

The setting for the Part One of the book is in rural India in the 1960s. Kaali is the downtrodden heroine who has been raped by Abha, a passing drunken salesman. Abha is pressured into marrying Kaali, a decision he regrets and ensures that her life remains subservient to him and his family. Four years later, in the hope of a successful future in England, Abha gets the necessary permits to immigrate to England and his mother, Devi, insisted that he takes Kaali and his daughter Karishma with him. The journey to England is by ship and during these three weeks, Abha is a transformed man. He is full of optimism for the future. They arrive in England and adjust to the new way of life. However, Abha begins to despair when things do not turn out as expected and begins to drink as before. Kaali, gives birth to a son and Abha is overjoyed that it is a boy.

Part Two of the book is about Karishma, Kari for short, who grows up in care in England. She is taken into an orphanage and moved from home to home. She develops a tough spirit and survival skills in the children's homes and takes her destiny into her own hands.

Preface

Like many people, it was my dream to one day write a book. Over the years it was a case of write, delete, write, delete. I was never satisfied. I worried about people's opinions at my amateurish efforts.

However, just over a year ago, I was taking a walk in the woods, pondering over my lack of effort and sheer laziness, when a story began to form in my mind. I had been compelled to write many times before, but this time it was more of a frenzy, a feeling which excited me. I went home and got straight ~~into~~ [work] typing ~~my story, (not my personal story!)~~. I had been reading tips from many authors on ~~Twitter~~ [Social Media] and the main advice I took on board was ~~not~~ to ~~stop and~~ correct, ~~that came later~~. So I ~~kept on writing~~ [Keep on writing / did] for about an hour or ~~so~~ [more], day ~~after day~~ [hours each] and felt thrilled as I saw my word count grow.

~~It~~ [The Frenzy] lasted about a month. I was back in my world of 'not good enough', 'badly written' and so forth. I did not write for another couple of months because I no longer knew where my story was going. The fact was obvious; it was not going anywhere simply because I had stopped writing.

I cautiously started correcting my work to get back into the mood and ended changing many things. But at least I was confronting my reluctance to continue. Again tips from my friend, Twitter, such as write for at least fifteen minutes a day. Read when you are not writing. The advice was endless. When I could finally see my work moving forward, I invited my daughter to start reading it for feedback at the same time, dreading the response. She was a blessing, because as she read my book, she demanded more chapters, 'Mum! I want to know what happens next!'

Excited, I now persevered, although my deadline of finishing the book in six months had long passed. I then took the courage to ask my sister if she would be willing to read and proofread my effort. Again, an amazing and motivating response. Aishah and Naleefa, with their kind and gentle critic, definitely helped me to reach my goal, I hope they realise how much it meant to me.

PART ONE

She lies low,
Bending with the wind
Until she can take no more.

CHAPTER 1

It began with my violent conception in a rural village, with voluptuous undulating hills, a sparkling river with silver confetti, deceptive of the impoverished lives of those that lay within. It was on the outskirts of the dusty town of Kurnool in the state of Andhra Pradesh, the small hamlet lay hidden, ~~a mere bus ride away.~~ My tiny, fragile mother, Kaali, still a mere child at the ripening age of fifteen, was raped by the oaf like, cumbersome frame of Abha. He spotted her with his lecherous, bloodshot eyes and violated her body on a velvety patch behind a sprouting bush.

Kaali had been walking to the banks of the river Krishna for its pure water, to quench the thirst of her siblings, balancing the earthen pot on her head, resting it just over the glossy knot of hair. Her neck

and shoulders poised with grace and strength, her
dark skin glowing from the sun's rays. He [Aloka] had been
driving, drunk as a skunk, veering his metal heap
into the dirt road looking for trouble. Tragically, he
found my gentle mother, paralysed by fear,
incapable of protecting herself from his groping
hands. He was driven by lust and an insane desire to
ravage this dark, silken waif. Her limp, skeletal
body was thrown, assaulted by the sheer urgency of
the assailant's need. Her stunned form was unable to
fight back the strength of the bulk which
overshadowed her. Her mind shut down sickened by
the breath and grunting of the vile man.
He heaved himself on top of her, pressing down on
her lips, tugging forcefully at her knot of hair,
sniggering in drunken ecstasy. The earthen pot
rolled away, smashed into a rock and lay broken.
Kaali too lay broken, in shock, in pain until the
brute eased himself off her and scrambled back onto
his feet.

Unfortunately, her widely respected father [Odda] was
walking back from his various business negotiations
where his self- importance was more apparent than
the profits from his trade. His purposeful
wanderings and sly practices kept the other villagers
in check. He froze when he saw his daughter
crawling out from behind a bush. A strange man
stood laughing at her side as he pulled up his

trousers. His shock and disgust to find his dutiful, but usually invisible daughter in an uncompromising position had his mind momentarily paralysed. He screamed with revulsion at the thought of this abomination immersed in vulgar behaviour. Kaali's body shuddered as if the bones would just give way and collapse in a heap. Her mind and body registered nothing of her father's presence or that of Abha. She could barely hear anything above the screaming in her head, and the thudding of her heartbeat, and the blood rushing in her ears.

Her father, Odda, ranted in decibels he had not known he was capable of, moving forward slapping and kicking Kaali in murderous anger and it seemed that half the village came running from their homes to witness the drama. Kaali, debased by a strange and now assaulted by her father was at the point of losing her mind.

The cowardly Abha, zipped up his trousers and held up his hands as if to surrender, pleading that it was Kaali who had followed him and lured him and that his only sin was that he had been too easily lead astray. He scolded the father for allowing his daughter to walk freely, unchaperoned and dressed in such an immodest manner, although not an inch of her flesh was visible other than her dark, oval face, her hands and soiled feet.

The inflamed Odda dragged Kaali by her unkempt

hair, while the rest of the company, eager to be part of the drama, also grabbed the girl and the drunken man and dragged them back to the village, scolding only her, all the way. The wild mayhem followed the sinful pair. The facts were obvious, the girl had sinned and the man could not be wholly blamed.

It was incumbent upon each villager that they had a story to tell of the shame which had befallen the Odda family and their own heroic contribution back in their own households and a warning to the girls that still lived. The women were peering through the windows and clustered through the partly open doorways.

My poor, dumb mother was thrown into a corner where she sat, violently trembling, tears streaming down her muddy cheeks. She was not treated as the victim or justly given the opportunity to relate the true version of events. She was guilty without question. Her mother and sisters appeared, all furious of the incredulous shame she had brought upon the family and looked at her in disgust. They took it in turns to slap her and spit on her, screaming unheard of obscenities.

Rape was not an uncommon crime but rarely reported because it was not acceptable that a girl did not shoulder the blame. The offender was nearly always the girl and the men's actions were generally ignored or justified. In this hamlet, the men made the laws as handed to them by the gods and there was no question of a man being pronounced guilty of rape.

Hence, Abha was offered a seat at a table out in the open, in front of their home, with refreshments of tea and biscuits. The sly father had quickly grasped the good fortune of the situation and had already, in his mind planned the dispatch of the burden that was this unwanted daughter. He snapped his fingers for more tea to serve to his guest, offering him cigarettes and tactfully questioning him about his family and his livelihood.

Abha, always ready to brag, spouted out the grossly inflated success of his various businesses and the size of his house in Madras. He was on his way back from securing a land deal when he had simply taken a wrong turning only to have been taken advantage of by his daughter. He professed his embarrassment of being so weak in his ability to resist the temptation that had been laid before him.

The noble elders of the village sat in an untidy circle outside the hut with the father and male relatives, all in intense discussion. Most of the villagers were related in some sense or another. The women of the village lingered at doorways and windows, whispering to each other, enjoying the unfolding drama at the Odda household. Those who had borne sons, stood proudly with their arms folded, self-righteous and unforgiving. The verdict was pre-written and there were no doubts that Kaali had committed a huge crime and sinned in the eyes of the gods and brought shame upon the family, the community and the whole village.

Odda was in deep, secretive conversation with his conspirators to find a satisfactory solution to end the calamity. There was much whispering and nodding of heads. The local postmaster who served the village, acted as scribe and officiously made notes, sending Odda running into his house to search for documents. Abha was plied with more sweet tea, cake and his ego was massaged while he lounged carelessly smoking freshly rolled cigarettes.

Finally, Abha was approached by a group of the most senior of the villagers and a proposition was put forward. He was offered the hand of Kaali in marriage to take away immediately or they could not guarantee the fate that would befall her. Abha was horrified at the thought of having to take a village girl for a wife. She was poor, dark and now unclean. He vehemently shook his head and refused, stating that the brokers were in the process of looking for a wife for him already, someone from the city who would be fair with a big dowry.

Odda, sadly wringing his hands, explained that there was no future for her in the village and if she did not leave there would be several consequences. Firstly, she was most likely to be stoned and then probably hung if she was not already dead. The whole family would also be shunned by the village in fear of their daughters being influenced by her sisters. The anxious father stated that he would personally throw the remaining daughters into a well rather than risk repeating the shame. She was already dead to him and his family. He disowned her in a loud public proclamation and with crocodile tears and loud wailing, beating his chest, stated that his heart had been broken and would deny her existence henceforth. He bemoaned his lamentations to the gods to save him from the ruin of his family and cried out to the heavens that he had no money for dowries, no sons to protect them and his health was failing. His only solutions were to kill or sell his daughters. He was a broken man.

Abha had sobered somewhat and absorbed his rather uncompromising situation. His protestations were of no avail. He had been a drunken fool but a tiny prickle of conscience prevented him from walking away, leaving the girl and all her sisters at death's door, a painful death at that. He could not even remember what Kaali looked like such was his ignorance. But to be offered no dowry was such an insult. He started negotiating more favourable terms where he didn't just walk away with nothing more than an unwanted wife, but his rhetoric had no influence on the weeping father. The indignant

Odda flatly refused, saying that even if he was a millionaire, he would not pay a single cent for such a worthless and shameless daughter.

Abha was undeniably an extremely unpleasant character but not wanting blood on his hands, agreed to take Kaali as his wife proclaiming his innocence once again and trusting the gods would reward him for the generosity of his heart.
The wedding was of course a complete sham. Kaali, the child bride, was dragged from her cold, stone corner and forced to sit in front of a blazing fire, which had now been lit. She had no idea of what was happening to her but acknowledged her crime and was prepared to accept her punishment. She was still reeling from the shock of being raped, not even understanding and knowing what the violation of her young body had undergone.

Words were uttered by the elders and expressive

arms and hands flailed around as if to banish her from their presence rather than unite a couple in marriage. Abha then snapped his fingers and signalled her to rise up to a standing position where she cowed, still trembling, her gaze directed to the ground. Her face, hands and clothes were etched and stamped with the earth from beneath her. Her hair was mangled and wiry with twigs and dry leaves scattered as her bridal veil.

"Follow Me!" he barked and marched forward in horrified regret that he had agreed to this ridiculous marriage. She would be a useful servant in his home and nothing more. Not only had he got himself a dark, village girl but he had been given no dowry to guarantee a reputable future. Kaali's mother threw a bundle of clothes wrapped in an old blanket after her and walked away. Odda produced a piece of grubby paper, which appeared to be the only evidence of her birth along with the hastily produced marriage certificate. He was looking smug that he had finally got rid of a daughter without a dowry, one that he should have buried at birth. He had no affection for her and far as he was concerned she was dead to the family or worse still, she had never existed.

Kaali picked up the bundle and trotted after the man who had robbed and soiled her. Abha signalled her into the back seat of his car wondering what he was going to do with her. He felt quite repulsed by her pathetic frame and could not bear to touch her or even look at her. He rested his head on the steering wheel gathering his thoughts at the speed of events in the last few hours. It was sobering. He had to get home and produce this girl to his family, but it would as a servant not his wife. He was cross that somehow he had been trapped to accept this marriage.

"What's your name?" he shouted, irritated.
"Kaali" she replied in almost a whisper.
"You look filthy! Go and wash in the river. I can't take you home like this. Hurry up, you stupid fool!"
Kaali was eager to bathe and ran to the river as fast as her scrawny legs could carry her. She placed her bundle by the bank and walked straight into the water fully clothed, until she could just about touch the shingles on the river bed. She undid her scruffy knot and dipped her head underwater wishing she could just remain there forgotten. The coolness of the water calmed her mind. The current massaged her tiny frame. She swayed her legs and arms, treading water, willing every drop of contamination to flee her body. She took a smooth stone and rubbed her skin, gently and then increasingly

aggressively. She started sobbing, still not understanding the day's events but knowing that she had committed a huge sin and it would take a lifetime to gain repentance. She suddenly snapped out of her stupor and the all absorbing anguish she felt for her sisters. Fear gripped her as she remembered the waiting man. Her last wish was to disobey him, he who had taken her away from an unforgiving father and the punishment of death. She hurriedly changed her clothes and managed to tie her hair back as securely as possible with a piece of rag. She wrapped her wet clothes in the blanket and ran back to the car. She quietly slipped into the back seat and bowed her head.

"You took so long, idiot, and you don't look any better!" muttered Abha irritated.

CHAPTER 2

Abha started the angry engine, geared it into action and they moved forward over the erratic stony track, forward into their new life as husband and wife.

Abha could not have foreseen how his day was going to end or he probably would have stayed in bed or even in the temple meditating and praying for good fortune.

He mulled over as to how he was going to explain the arrival of the additional burden to the family, frustrated and angry with Kaali for having thrust herself into his life. This was not his plan for a marriage, Kaali was of lowly birth and an embarrassment. The alcohol and the sunshine had played tricks on his mind. His mother, especially, expected him to marry into a professional and wealthy family of good repute. There were many marriage brokers who were looking for the right girl, all eager to lay claim to a big fat commission. Marriage brokering was big business with families promoting their children's assets such as fair, beautiful and a good cook for the girls and qualified professional and successful businessman for the boys.

Abha knew it would be a huge tragedy for his mother and she could read him like a child's book knowing that there was more to the tale than a servant girl to help her out. He could see the benefit of an extra pair of hands to help his ailing mother. They had a constant stream of helping hands and a woman came regularly to do the laundry, but the general upkeep of the family home had been neglected. He had four brothers and no sisters and none of the brothers stayed long enough in the house other than to eat and sleep. His father was an ugly but charming rogue with unsavoury friends, who spent their days on earning money by dubious means and evenings smoking cigarettes, drinking alcohol, gambling and harassing women.

Abha, the eldest, took after his father both in looks and behaviour. But he had an element of responsibility when it came to taking care of his mother and the home. He envisaged a future of success and grandeur but his efforts were thwarted as he always managed to spend more than he earned. Thus, his income was spasmodic as any unlucky and over confident salesman's would be.

The two youngest brothers, Manish and Niraj, were still at school, immature and uninterested in the value of education. They studied very little and loitered at dusty corners with their unruly friends, having no ambition to attempt any task that was too trying. They had no role models to follow or guidance from the adults except the occasional command to go and study.

Ashok and Chetan, the remaining two brothers, neither academically inclined, had what was considered to be reasonably secure jobs. Ashok worked at a local restaurant as a kitchen porter, the perks being that he was able to sneak food home for his mother and also enjoy a good lunch daily as part of his pay. He was content with his lot and had no aspirations, although each day was a mindless stream of mundane actions with no challenges. Chetan had a tuktuk, so his flexible working hours meant that he could frequent the cinema and no one would know where he was at any given time. He aspired to be on the big screen one day. He would sing soulful love songs while manoeuvring his tuktuk through the dusty roads and lanes of the growing bustle of Kurnool. He would perform overly dramatic love scenes to his friends and family much to their amusement. He was a lovable and sensitive character unlike Abha and would get deeply upset if his father raised his voice to his mother, which was a frequent occurrence during his drunken evenings.

He would take Devi to visit relatives, shopping or just drive around to satisfy her inquisitive nature. She would ask to see a new house or extensions that was being built or the redecorations of any of their relatives or friends houses. Back at home she would gossip with the neighbours insulting the colours of the new paint or the sloppy building works.
She thrived on people's listening ears and her lamenting was of a dramatic version of her mostly imaginary daily woes. Devi had an air of arrogance for having given birth to five sons. This was overshadowed by the fragility of her existence with a man that drank too much and sons that achieved too little. Undoubtedly, the boys all cared for their mother. Anil knew that Devi would always lie to protect him and the family rather say anything against him for fear of shame and embarrassment. In their family and social network, Devi was looked up to with high regard and her audience would listen to her with respect and would not dare to utter a single

negative remark about Anil or her sons. She was wise enough to know that family and neighbours could not be trusted and within their four walls, there was a lot of cackling and gossip. If anyone deigned to mention a titbit or some nonsense, Devi would simply brush it aside laughing, "Yes, boys will be boys".

Devi was also the treasure of Anil's parents for giving birth to five handsome boys. They adored her and turned a blind eye to any misbehaviour by the boys knowing full well that their son had an unpleasant streak and often gave Devi a hard time. They too would defend any wrong doings by the boys and deny any irresponsibility of Anil. Hence the boys grew up with very little discipline or guidance, each feeling his way to the rights and wrongs of existence and Anil did as he pleased not answerable to anyone.

Abha pulled up in front of his relatively comfortable home. To have three bedrooms was a distinct sign of prosperity even if in reality there was not an abundance of food on the table.
"Get out and walk behind me. Don't talk. Don't make a fool of me!"
Kaali obeyed, still unsure as to what was happening except that her family had banished her because of her unforgivable sin. She was too shocked and

stunned to shed any more tears and tiptoed behind her master into her new existence. Her only stance was submission and acceptance and to spend her days repenting and serving her master dutifully.

"Ma! Ma! I'm home!" Abha wandered into the kitchen with Kaali practically crawling behind him, carrying her wet bundle. Her unsteady gait and bowed head gave her the persona of a drunken street beggar.
"I have brought home this servant girl. She can help you. Tell her to do whatever you want. I had to marry her to save her from death. Don't ask me any questions!" Abha reeled out his rehearsed introduction, clumsily tripping over the words 'had to marry'. He could feel the sweat on his face as his mother glared at him. He did not think any further comment would be wise and moved back towards the door to make a quick exit.

Devi looked at Kaali, knitting her eyebrows and called after Abha and stopped him in his tracks. "Your married her! This dirty street beggar! How much dowry did you get? Why didn't you talk with me and the family first? We would have found you a beautiful, fair girl with a big dowry and lot of jewellery and even maybe a house! This is just a beggar from the street! You must be mad!"
Kaali unflinchingly absorbed the fact that she was

Abha's wife. Her heart beat like the wings of a butterfly. The words rang like the clanging of temple bells in her ears. She felt naked and totally out of her depth to imagine that she could be a wife of this stranger, and without even a bangle to her name. She felt ashamed and disgusted with her appearance. Devi was right, she looked no better than a beggar off the street. She pulled her shawl further over her face, wanting to run and hide. She did not know how she would ever be able to repay this man who had stooped so low to take her as his wife, dark skinned, ugly and with no dowry or jewellery.

She knelt on the floor and kissed Devi's feet with overwhelming gratitude and mumbled blessings and her commitment to serve the family. She remained prostrated, pulling the shawl even tighter around her tiny, trembling body.
"Ma, don't worry about the dowry or anything but I'll talk about it later. I have to go now.
I still have work to do."
Abha escaped before his furious mother questioned him further.

Outside, Abha lit a cigarette, leant against his car, feeling very hard done by. The one whispered shadow of conscience to save her from death was now buried and abandoned forever. He was the ultimate victim of this mad day and Kaali, the perpetrator who had slyly invaded his life and his home. He would make sure she suffered for her crime and find a way to get rid of her. He regretted agreeing to anything and would have happily stoned her to death himself rather than have her living under his roof. His mother's words rang in his ears. She had always busied herself with the various proposals, rejecting many which she felt were beneath their status. He too had aspirations of marrying a fair, beautiful girl from a wealthy, noble family. At the very least, he would have received a house as dowry. He stamped on the smouldering butt and drove off in a rage.

CHAPTER 3

Devi looked disgustedly at Kaali who was still sat prostrated on the floor before her and sighed. She looked like a pile of dirty laundry waiting to be scrubbed clean.
"Hmm! What am I to do with you? How did you manage to get my dear son to marry you? You have made a big mistake if you think you are going to be treated like a queen, I will make sure I find out the truth and get you thrown into prison!"
Kaali sat trembling on the floor. She had no defence to put forward and would have been quite happy to be thrown into a prison or a well. She was not deserving of a life of any joy or happiness.

Devi got up from her chair with difficulty and without another word, limped out of the kitchen through the barn door that lead into the street. She wanted to scream with the shame and embarrassment she felt. How would she be able to face her relatives and neighbours. She would be the laughing stock in her neighbourhood.

Kaali still sat on the floor, unsure if she should follow or stay in the kitchen. Finally, she slowly got up and followed Devi, head bowed. She accepted that whatever she did was going to be wrong and she would have to face the consequences. Devi stopped and slowly turned around. She looked at Kaali and shook her head vigorously, growling through gritted teeth, "Get back inside! Don't ever come out here again! I don't know what fool this son of mine has brought home. What did you do that he had to marry you!"
She descended into a torrent of accusations.
"You come here with a bundle of old rags. You village girls, you have no shame. You will bring shame to this well respected family. You trick and curse our boys with your witchcraft and look at you! You're so dark and have slanting crafty eyes. He couldn't have married you for your beauty!"

Kaali remained silent, head bowed, ashamed and embarrassed by her appearance and wishing she had remained underwater, or allowed her father to throw her into a well or even better, that he had buried her at birth as he had often told her.

"For my dear good hearted son's sake, I will let you stay in my house. But if you ever disobey me or bring any shame to our family, I will beat you until every bone in your body is broken!"

Kaali whimpered her humble gratitude, her voice barely a whisper.

A feint shadow of pleasure passed across Devi's face. The girl would be of some help and she would be able to get rid of the washer woman and the random, untrustworthy servant girls that her son would bring home. Keeping house and the constant cooking was no longer of any interest to Devi who would rather sit with tea and sympathy with her false friends. However, she had to find a way of saving face with inquisitive family and neighbours. It would never do for it to be known that her eldest son had married a beggar girl far beneath him. They would be the laughing stock for miles around and beyond. Bad news always travelled fast. All the visits they would get once word got around would be full of reassurances and sympathy. Devi knew that out of earshot, the hypocrites would be rejoicing in her calamity. There was always jealousy, mistrust and back stabbing and Devi was the Queen of gossip.

Devi hobbled back to the kitchen and sat herself in her large wooden chair. She felt very comfortable in her throne where she looked down at all and had a vantage point where nothing escaped her eyes. And now she had this servant girl to do the work, where previously she just had the occasional home help. "Put down your dirty bundle in that corner and listen to everything I say. I'm too old and sick to keep repeating myself. I don't want you to spend your time being lazy. Take rice and lentils from those sacks and start cleaning them. These rogues in the shops always put in some tiny stones and charge more. You can't trust anyone any more. Thank goodness for my dear sons and good husband who look after me so well. We are a very highly respected family. Don't ever talk to anyone and turn us into laughing stocks! You think that you're the first servant girl I ever had!? Oh no, I've had to get rid of many because they were too lazy or they were thieves. So don't think that you're here to be treated like e queen just because you slyly married into a good family!"

Devi rambled on with complaints and instructions and Kaali swayed to her tune bent on escaping any kind of displeasure and to serve Devi and the household with all her heart. Neighbours glanced in through the open door, curious about the new arrival. Devi assured them that Kaali was not her choice but had bewitched her son into marriage and had come with nothing. All they had was another mouth to feed and she could only praise the gods for the goodness of her son's heart. The neighbours shook their heads and offered sympathy. They commented on the girl's suspicious appearance and warned Devi to be careful.

All the time, Kaali was occupied with lighting a fire with chopped wood, cooking the meals, cleaning and scrubbing everything she touched after use, making endless teas for the growing bandwagon that streamed in. She massaged Devi's knees when she complained of pain. She fetched water from the tap outside, always fearful lest a drop of water or grain of rice was spilt. She was sent out to scrub the outside toilets and the concreted back yard as if she had contaminated it.

This lifestyle was not much different to her previous home where as the eldest, unwanted daughter, her duty was to take care of her parents, the household and her younger siblings. She would cook, sew, clean and take the blame for every chore left undone.

Evening was drawing and one by one the sons were returning. Ashok returned with a loaf of bread given to him by the restaurant owner and some masala dosais he had managed to hide from the kitchen. "Abha is married!!" he exclaimed in disbelief. He examined Kaali's downcast face and was puzzled at his brother's choice but said nothing further.

Chetan was in good humour after seeing the latest release at the cinema and lived in a romantic world where love was blind and everyone was beautiful.

"Ah Ma! This is good for you. Someone to keep you company and help you."

"I have plenty of company. They all come here and drink my tea as if I was the manager of a tea plantation! But the girl will be useful but Abha could have done much better for himself. He is too soft hearted."

Chetan although in complete disagreement with his mother's complimentary comments, chose not to antagonise her, "Where is he anyway? Shouldn't he be spending time with his new bride?"

"Chetan! Stop talking rubbish! Look at her! She has tricked him into marriage. He will now stay out more than ever! "

Kaali, now used to the constant verbal abuse which attacked her as if she was invisible, remained silently apologetic for her intrusion. There was very little difference from her previous existence with her father and mother. She shrunk within herself, always following instructions, laying the table for the meal and staying as invisible as possible, silently gliding around the kitchen.

Ashok and Chetan helped themselves rapidly, keen to try out their sister-in-law's cooking.

"Very nice!" said Chetan. "Aren't you going to eat?"

Kaali shook her head, embarrassed to be even asked.

"You must be waiting for your husband, right!?" he laughed.

Kaali sensed the kindness in his voice. But she was unable to smile or reply. She held back all emotion and looked down demurely.

Devi shattered the moment, "Chetan! I don't want you laughing and joking with this chit of a girl! She is not to be trusted! Do you understand!? Poor Abha did not enter this stupid marriage of his own free will, it was her trickery and the only thing tasty on this table is the masala dosais you brought with your hard working hands ".

Chetan was stunned at his mother's aggression and exchanged glances with Ashok, who simply shrugged his shoulders. He avoided confrontation and did not think his brother's marriage was his business. The meal was very tasty but decided that he wouldn't mention it for it would surely infuriate his mother further.

Manish and Niraj came in laughing and punching each other playfully.

"Where have you two been? School finished ages

ago!" yelled Devi lovingly.

"I was in the library studying, but Niraj was chasing the girls in the playground!" squealed Manish.

"He's lying, ma, I was in the library and Manish was the one chasing the girls. He is such a liar!"

Devi was getting irritated. "I don't want to hear anymore nonsense. Sit and eat your dinner."

The lanky, adolescent boys settled down, still mock fighting until they noticed the dark shadowy figure moving around the fireplace.

Devi shot them a warning glance. "Eat your dinner and don't ask any questions. I am tired of everyone asking me the same things over and over again. "

Devi started sobbing, bringing out her crumpled hanky to wipe away the invisible tears. The boys all ate silently knowing that their mother's mood would very quickly swing to another mode if left alone.

Then in came Anil, the man of the house. He had already heard the rumours of the new inhabitant of his household. Devi and the boys all remained silent. He eyed the dark girl.

"So Abha has brought home a wife!"

Anil looked at her and laughed out aloud.

"Don't be so scared. You will be like our daughter. We have too many useless sons."

He then turned his attention to Devi, "Why is she in the kitchen on her first day as a new bride? We must treat her like our daughter! "

Devi remained silent.

"Sit at the table, child. Get this girl some food she doesn't look as if she's eaten for a month!"

Devi stared at Kaali, her eyes black with anger. Kaali vigorously shook her head and remained standing in the corner with her eyes downcast. Anil shrugged his shoulders and piled his plate with enough food to absorb the beer in his gut. He had other more pressing issues such as to how to fund his drinking, smoking and other excesses.

CHAPTER 4

The boys had all retired after some confusion over sleeping arrangements as now it seemed obvious that Abha would need a room to himself. Abha, himself arrived late into the night to find everyone had gone to bed except for Kaali who remained seated in a corner on the kitchen floor. His meal remained covered on the table.
"You can't sit here all night, you stupid girl."
He had already eaten but after many beers he was ready for a second meal. He sat and slobbered over the curry and asked, "Did you cook this?"
Kaali nodded, always looking to the ground, fearful of any eye contact. When he had finished, she cleared and washed the plate, wiped down the table and sat back on the floor.
"Tea!" he ordered.
Once again, Kaali moved around quickly and

quietly, desperate not to displease her husband.

He sat wondering what he was to do with this burden he had acquired. His anger would rise at his predicament, totally adamant that the blame lay at her feet. He had been a fool to agree to this marriage and should have just let her father throw her in the well. On the positive side, he could see that clearly she could deal with all the household chores and relieve his mother of the pressure. It would also save him money and the nuisance of always having to find servants to help his easily displeased mother.

The thought of sharing a bed with Kaali was repulsive but he had to put up a front for the time being for his mother's sake, he did not particularly care about the opinions of others. He signalled her to collect her bundle and follow him to the bedroom. Kaali was trembling. She felt her knees wobbling and she struggled to drag each leg forward. Abha shut the bedroom door and took a deep breath. The last thing on his mind was to lay a finger on this girl ever again. He threw a pillow on the floor and motioned Kaali to sleep there.

Kaali made an inward deep grateful sigh of relief that she could curl up and rest her weary body and mind. She covered herself with the old blanket that was used to wrap her bundle and fell into a deep black hole where the nightmares kept recurring. Abha lay silent, thoughtful, scheming, searching for a solution to free himself and still be a hero. The love and respect he had for his mother prevented him from acting too hastily. His mind went in circles until sleep finally overtook his shallow dreams.

Kaali fell into a light slumber only after she sensed that Abha had drifted into a deep sleep. It was rare that she ever slept through the night or missed a single sound or movement. She could hear his snores which were gently resounding through the whole house.

The first morning light was peeping through the windows. She took her clothes and went silently outside to wash herself the best she could at the outside tap which seemed to be the only source for running water. In the kitchen, she had the firewood ready and everything needed to make breakfast and tea for the family. She was grateful that she had been the main charge who had to carry out all the household duties in her village home, it had taught her much about frugality and compromise. She could lose herself in the domestics always caring for others. The intense pleasure she got from serving others numbed the pain and regret she felt for herself.

She heard voices, as one by one, the family rose to face the day. Kaali busied herself with making breakfast. Devi hobbled into the kitchen, wiping her face with her crumpled hanky.

"Why haven't you made breakfast yet? Don't you know the boys have to go to school! I knew you were a lazy one. I will become more ill having to chase after you!"

Kaali moved faster churning out the idli and curry. She was eternally grateful to have a serving role and to be of use in a family that had provided a roof over her head. She constantly reminded herself of her unworthiness and their charity when even a passing breeze of fatigue crossed her thoughts.

The boys trooped in one after the other, scoffing down their breakfast and talking loudly as if they had no care in the world. Her own family, which consisted of four girls, was relatively quieter as they all lived in gratitude of their father letting them live where so many others had perished. Her youngest sister, Indira, was the only one who received preferential treatment because not only was she fair and beautiful but also quick to grasp literacy. She was the only one who was encouraged to study. Her father and mother believed that she would marry well if they took good care of her. There was a total disregard to the feelings of the remaining three daughters. Nor was there any guilt in showing such open favouritism. Indira seemed oblivious to the unfair treatment of her sisters and only revelled in being the shining beacon of the family and their fortunes.

Devi ate her breakfast alongside her sons, pulling faces as if it was an effort to eat food prepared by such an abomination.
"Is Abha still sleeping?" she asked Kaali.
Kaali nodded as she cleared away plates and started to wash up.

The boys had all disappeared after a quiet whispered thank you to Kaali. They knew their mother could be a bit of a tyrant and always anxious about the family reputation. But they accepted this as the normal behaviour of most parents and especially the pressure upon their mother having to keep their father in check.

Devi sat at the table sipping her masala tea. Her mind confused and knotted of what the future may hold. She dreaded the visit she knew she would get from her husband's family as well as her own about this dreadful and unfortunate marriage. She knew she had to make plans to make this girl more presentable to save at least some embarrassment. Also she did not want to be seen as someone who would ill-treat another no matter what the circumstance.

Abha drifted into the kitchen followed by Anil. "Good morning, Ma! How are your knees this morning?"
Kaali rushed to get tea for them and laid plates for breakfast. Abha ignored her presence and continued talking to his mother. But Anil was still in a jolly mood, "Well, son, so you have brought home a wife!"
Abha looked upwards in annoyance but Anil carried on, "We must have a party to celebrate!"
"No Pa! No party! I'm too busy with work!"
Devi interrupted, "All the babus are coming this evening. They've been listening to all the gossip."
Abha frowned and looked down into his tea. He had no solution.
"You have to be here when they come. I can't manage this on my own. It is your duty to be here."
Anil laughed, "Excellent! We'll have a party tonight! I'll be back home early!"
Abha also conceded "Ok Ma, I'll come home early from work. We'll order food from somewhere. Don't worry, it will be alright. "
Abha finished his breakfast and left after giving his mother a fleeting hug, which always lifted her spirits.

"Have you eaten?" Devi asked Kaali.
Kaali shook her head.
"What, you want to die of starvation and cost me more money for a funeral! For goodness sake, you stupid fool, eat some food and drink some tea!" Devi wobbled out the door holding her head in both hands for the headache this girl was causing her. Devi had been roaming around the neighbourhood relating her woes to anyone who would listen. Eventually, her stomach needing refuelling, she found herself back in her kitchen to find Kaali scrubbing the floor. She had never seen it looking so good.

"If there is any idli left from this morning, I'll have it for lunch. It's no point wasting. You have to learn to make the right amount or I have to keep eating the leftovers. We don't have money to throw especially with an extra mouth to feed!"
Kaali, warmed the idli and curry and prepared tea for Devi. She kept busy cleaning and wiping so that Devi would not see her idle.
"We have important visitors this evening. You have come with nothing! Is there anything decent in that dirty bundle of yours?" questioned Devi vehemently.
Kaali meekly shook her head.
"I don't know what to do with you." Devi rubbed her eyes and brow, sighing. "This should never have

happened."

"Eat your lunch then come to my room. I'm going to have a lie down. Without my afternoon rest, my blood pressure will be too high. And with all the trouble you have brought upon me, I'm surprised that I'm not already dead after a heart attack!"

Kaali finished off the last of the idli. She never tasted the food, just ate it. She drank her tea, gulping lest anyone should see her. She never sat at the table but on the kitchen floor in her corner, just as she had done in her own village home. After clearing up, she cautiously made her way to Devi's room. She had never dared to venture near the master bedroom. She kept herself mainly in the kitchen or in the backyard, always delighted to find a new corner or item to scrub or polish. She found it therapeutic to scrub and thrived on the admonishments to make herself feel worthy of her new family.

CHAPTER 5

Kali tapped on Devi's door.
"Get in here, girl. I told you to come didn't I? Why are you so slow at everything?"
Kali gingerly stepped in walking onto a plush Persian rug.
"Tomorrow, I want you to take this rug outside and give it a good beating otherwise I'll give you a good beating! There are so many things I can't do anymore. When I was newly married, I worked hard and looked after my husband very well. Not like you so slow and lazy."
Kali listened intently, making a mental note that she must look after her husband with every ounce of strength as was her duty. He had married her against all the odds and she knew she would for ever be grateful to him.

Devi opened her huge oak wardrobe. Kali inwardly gasped. She had never seen so many possessions for one person.

Devi sighed once again, "I have to dress you in my old clothes just so that I don't get embarrassed in front of our relations. After giving birth to five sons, hardly any of these old blouses fit me."

Kali remained motionless, her gaze knotted into the twine of the rug. Devi pulled out a sari and blouse in a deep red shade with a green border.

"Put this on and let me see if I make you look better just for this evening at least. Goodness knows if anything can make you look good enough to be my son's wife!"

Kali felt shy and not sure how to try on these clothes in front of Devi. She had only secretly tried on her mother's saris when she had gone out with her father and Indira. The three sisters would try on the few saris that her mother had while taking it in turns to keep watch for their return.

"Take off your clothes and put on this underskirt and blouse! No point in being shy now after you have taken the trouble to catch my son!"

Kali deftly put on the underskirt like a tent round her neck, removing her salwar kameez from underneath. She then put on the blouse lowering the underskirt as she did so.

Devi handed her the sari "don't you dare dirty my clothes; I can't believe that I'm even doing this. But

remember I'm only doing this for my Abhu so don't get any ideas that you're going to sit around like a rani and help yourself to my clothes and jewellery!" Kaali listened attentively and nodded obediently.
"At least save a little of the shame I feel. Make sure that when they go, you put everything back in my cupboard safely. I have kept everything safely all these years, I don't want you to spoil my things!"
Kali gently handled the chiffon and draped the sari as best she could. In her tiny frame, and forlorn gaze, she looked like a child bride in mourning.
"Sit down!"
Kali sat in front of the dressing table.
Devi astonishingly proceeded to unravel her hair and brush it through.
"At least it's clean. I hope you don't have any tiny creatures running around in your head or I will throw you out of the kitchen door"

Kaali sat motionless. Devi, constantly muttering, managed to tidy Kaali's hair into a neat plait that fell down to her waist. She inserted a couple of studded pins into each side. She dived back into the wardrobe and brought out a pendant which she fastened round her neck and placed two bangles on each arm. She suddenly looked horrified "Why are your ears not pierced!!"
Kaali looked down onto her lap. She was feeling extremely uncomfortable, firstly to be at the mercy

of Devi and the fact that no one had ever dressed her up like this before. Devi, getting increasingly flustered, and finally after a lot of rummaging, produced a pair of clip on earrings.
"Stand up! Let me see you properly"
Kaali stood up. She couldn't quite grasp what was happening to her. Deep in her disturbed mind, she wished that Abha would approve.
"You will never be beautiful, but you'll do. Now go to your room and sit and wait until Abu Comes back. Don't make anything dirty."

Kaali escaped to Abha's bedroom and sat gingerly on the edge of the bed. She dared not move. It was like being a dream maharani for an eternal moment. She had no ill opinions of Devi or Abha. She knew she was unworthy of their attention and kindness. She desperately wanted to please them and be worthy of their generosity. She felt like a fool having no intelligence or possessions.
She started at the opening of the door as Abha walked in. He looked at her and walked silently out again, pausing to take a second glance. Their eyes met briefly, Abha with an uncomfortable acknowledgment of approval and Kaali with an unintentional allure.

Devi walked in and threw some sandals at her.
"Put these on. Doesn't matter if they don't fit. You

won't be moving at all. You will sit where I tell you to and don't speak, just nod your head. Make sure you kiss their feet when they come and show some respect."

Devi was about to leave when she heard voices. "They are here. Come quickly and sit in the corner at the end of the sofa."

Kaali slipped her bare feet into the sandals and shuffled into the living room and sat in her assigned corner. The exuberant voices flowed into the lounge.

"You little devil, Abu, you slowly sneaked off and got married. And here I've been waiting all this time for a wedding invitation."

"Real scoundrel!! I hope she can cook well. Maybe you'll stay at home more instead of gallivanting!"

"Oh Abu will never change; he is just like his father. Maybe he will have five sons as well."

"In that case, we better not stay for too long, you have busy times ahead!"

"Stop it, Arju, you mustn't talk like that!" replied his wife laughing.

The family all jaunted into the living room to find the demurely sitting Kaali sitting on the edge of the sofa. Kaali rose and dropped to her knees to kiss the feet of the merry band.

"Get up, child. We are very happy to meet you on this happy occasion."

Arju helped her up and she walked slowly backwards to her seat with head bowed and heart beating.

"What a sweet girl even though she is a little dark. But the young people nowadays don't seem to worry about all that."

Arju agreed. "What does it matter fair or dark. As long as she is a good wife and gives him many sons. But you must fatten her up, she's very thin."

Abha winced at the continuous reference to future sons. The thought of ever having to lay a finger on her again brought waves of revulsion and disgust. The group, even Devi, enjoyed much banter at the couple's expense much to the embarrassment of Abha and Kaali.

They munched on savoury titbits and cake. Downed umpteen cups of tea made by Devi and the servant girl who had been brought in for the evening. She refused to let Kaali get up or help in any way much to both their discomfort.

Anil never arrived and no one questioned his absence.

Finally, they all left even more jovially then when they had arrived.

Devi looked at Kaali, "take my things off. The kitchen needs to be cleaned."

Kaali on cue, swiftly went to Devi's room and got back into her glad rags, which more comfortable, like her second skin. To be decked in finery was a painful reward which she did not deserve. She placed the jewellery and hairpins carefully on the dressing table and the sandals by the stool.

She scuttled into the safety of the kitchen, with an excitement within she had not experienced before, she put her heart and soul into the cleaning. She felt at peace being allowed to serve and care for this family who had taken her in. She had no one else after being disowned by her own family. Strangely this did not trouble her too much, her only regret that she had not served her parents with more commitment and care. Instead of being punished for her crime and guilt, she found herself being rewarded with this new jolly family and a new home. It was a hard existence in the sense that she knew in her heart she would never be worthy enough.

CHAPTER 6

The arduous days melted into weeks and the weeks into months. Kaali was passing time in an almost hypnotic state where she moved silently and her only thoughts and actions were to address the needs of others. Her words were minimal and only when necessary. She avoided eye contact at all times, but was quick to sense when Devi or Abha needed extra pampering or if they found her presence irritating.

The moods and conversation never changed. Devi would continuously bemoan the misfortune of having such an unworthy daughter-in-law, Abha would never acknowledge her presence or thank her for any meal or the continuous housework or laundry that Kaali had now undertaken for the whole family. The fact that Devi was now a lady of leisure had bypassed everyone's attention. The young boys just accepted that their shirts got washed and ironed and food was on the table. There was no drama, just a quiet peaceful magic.

If anyone spoke to Kaali, they never called her by name. It was most probable that no one really knew her name. Even Abha had never uttered her name after that first fateful day when he had questioned her. Anil drifted in and out of the house, eyeing Kaali with a glint in his eye. She would blend into the shadows and avoid being alone in the kitchen with him. Since his initial welcome, she felt his presence was like an ominous cloud.

Abha returned home one day at an exceptionally late hour knowing that Kaali would just be sitting in the kitchen waiting for him. He threw a bag at her. "I don't want you dressing like a beggar in this house."
Kaali looked in the bag the next morning and saw that Abha had bought her three separate outfits and a pair of sandals. Her heart pounded that he should do this for her and from that day forwards she made much effort to keep herself looking clean, neat and tidy so that she would not look offensive to his eyes. Devi however was keen eyed and not much passed her notice. She was clear that Kaali slept on the floor as by chance she saw a pillow and blanket wrapped neatly in a corner. But she also noticed the

slight swelling of Kaali's stomach and the lack of appetite and energy that appeared to have befallen this ugly duckling. There was a secret bloom and calmness in her gaze.

Kaali never complained, she never shirked her duties and kept the house clean, massaged Devi's legs every morning and listened to her constant carping.

"Are you pregnant?" Boomed Devi one morning out of the blue.

Kaali looked horrified not understanding Devi's question. Devi started laughing out loud.

"You really are a bigger fool than I thought! Don't you know that you're going to have a baby? Abha will have to take you to the doctor to get you checked."

Kaali touched her stomach as realisation dawned on her. The memory of the violent encounter returned to her with a savagery. Her face crumpled as she felt the broken woman she truly was.

"What's the matter with you, idiot!! You're not the first woman to have a baby. You should be grateful that my son took pity on you and married you!"

Kaali pulled herself together and continued to massage Devi's legs. Her head throbbed and the nausea was trapped in her throat. Her chest tightened and she already felt pity for the unwelcome child growing inside her. She felt dirty

and thought back to the river and hated her
cowardice for not remaining underwater.
She hated herself even more for feeling this way
when she should be feeling gratitude that she had
been taken in by the man whose life she had ruined.

Before retiring to bed that evening, Abha looked in
at the kitchen door and said,
"You have to see a doctor tomorrow. Be ready to
leave at 10."

When she eventually went to the bedroom she found
he was still awake, sitting up in bed reading the
papers. Kaali slithered along the wall and crumpled
onto the floor laying her head on the pillow. He
switched off the light and turned his back on her.
She waited for his snores but sensed that he was
lying awake and felt repulsed by her inexplicable
longing for his touch. She was angry with herself
for causing anxiety and expense to her husband and
would rather have been left to her own devices and
deal with her own pain.

Abha's mind was meandering into the past, cursing
himself for not walking away from that obnoxious
village and its inhabitants. It was true that she was
obedient and took care of his mother and all the
domestic needs, but he felt he was being unfairly
punished for a stupid moment. He had envisaged a

future of a romantic meeting with a beautiful, fair girl. He knew that his family would have negotiated a good dowry, a large house at the very least. There would have been celebrations and parties. Instead he was entombed in the fate of an unwanted chattel without joy and laughter buried in the dark corner of his room. And now, she was with child. He felt disgusted. He had made an appointment with the doctor to appease his mother, she was eager to have a grandson and he knew that although she would never admit this to anyone, she liked having the girl in the house. Every time he saw her, he felt a huge surge of anger. Every meal she put in front of him, he ate with resentment. He had not heard her utter a single word unless prompted and was both irritated and grateful for her demeanour. She was either busy cooking, cleaning or sitting in the darkest corner with a veil covering her hair as she bowed low. If she happened to be eating or drinking when he entered, she would stop straight away and not touch her meal or drink until he had left. She would put aside her needs and attend to his first or start cleaning the sooty stove so that her back was turned to him and he would not have to look at her.

Abha knew that her basic needs had to be met to avoid gossip from the community. His mother made sure of that. Devi spoke many an unkind word to Kaali and about Kaali but forcefully prompted Abha to buy clothes for the girl, take her to the doctor and now she even expected him to buy her a wedding ring.

"What will people say, that you are such a stingy man who treats his wife like an untouchable?" He would never be able to tell anyone, especially his mother, the true circumstances of his predicament but fortunately after the first day, she never even asked.

CHAPTER 7

Kaali sat in the back row of the waiting room as directed by Abha. He sat in the front row after discussion with the receptionist insisting on a female doctor only. To his disdain he had to attach his name to the girl's as a married couple.
"Mrs Kaali Chetti, please come forward."
Kaali jumped off her seat in embarrassment at the sound of her new strange name. Abha beckoned with a click of his fingers, without a backward glance and marched forward while Kaali mutely trailed behind. He directed her into the treatment room and went back to his seat.
"Good morning, Mrs Chetti, Congratulations, to both you and your husband. I can see that you seem very worried and shy. But please relax. I just want to check that all is in order."
A nurse stood by and proceeded to take her blood

pressure and blood samples. Kaali simply slumped into her rag doll demeanour to allow her body to be assaulted without her mental presence. The doctor then gave her a bottle and directed her to the toilets and asked her to produce a sample.

She could only manage a small quantity of dark yellow pungent liquid, which was taken away swiftly to be tested. The doctor frowned as she progressed with each stage. She asked Kaali to lie on the examination bed and raised her dress to examine her stomach. Kaali followed instructions without any complaint or comment.

"When did you have your last period?"

Kaali shrugged and looked away. She was not accustomed to discussing her personal bodily functions and menstruation was something she had stumbled upon and struggled with, with no guidance from her mother. Silence was always the best answer.

"Are you feeling frightened? You're very young! Your papers say you're 20, but you don't seem more than 15! Parents are far too protective these days and just give the girls in marriage without telling them anything!"

Dr Shivani looked at Kaali sadly.

"Does it hurt when you go to the toilet?"

Kaali shook her head not daring to mention the agonising burning sensations that passed through her body.

"Well, I'm going to prescribe some antibiotics both for your sake and the baby's. It appears that you are probably about three to four months pregnant already. I'm also going to arrange an appointment for a scan so we can determine the date and check that baby is doing well."

Kaali shook her head vigorously. What did the date matter and she would take care of everything herself. The undue excessive attention made her feel uncomfortable and guilty of the pressure it would put upon her husband and his mother.

Dr Shivani sighed. "Well I'll recommend it in a letter and you and your husband can decide. But I strongly advise you to return for a scan."

Kaali adjusted her clothing and slowly walked out with her now fixed stoop, pulling the veil over her head. Abha saw her from the corner of his eyes, a dark shrouded pathetic figure. To be seen with her embarrassed him and he walked out while she trotted to keep up with him in case she got lost. The nurse came running after, "Mr & Mrs Chetti, here is the prescription for the antibiotics."

Abha froze and turned around. Kaali stopped, not sure if she should turn and go back to the nurse. She could feel Abha's wrath enveloping her even at a distance. He brushed past and took the prescription and letter, "thank you, nurse."

They returned to the car silently.

Outside at the house, Abha grunted at Kaali to get out and then drove off irritated by the forthcoming burden. She felt acutely uncomfortable by all the fuss and attention, she just wanted to lie quietly on her own, to pass through life unnoticed and ignored. But there was work to be done and meal preparations to be carried out and most importantly to ensure that Devi did not see her idling. In the kitchen, she first prostrated before Devi as usual and then proceeded to get all the ingredients together for the evening meal, cleaning around her as she busied herself with non-existent dirt.
"Before you start, massage some ointment into my legs. The pain is so bad, must be this damp weather and all this worry I have with family. You have increased my worry a thousand fold! I don't know why God has punished me like this!" Devi drifted on with her complaints and protests about the life of suffering that had been served to her despite her being a good woman who had taken care of her husband and sons.

Kaali warmed the pungent balm in some hot water and sat down with bended knee and gently massaged Devi's legs, easing the pain and soothing Devi's impish mind.
"No point asking you what the doctor said, you're too stupid to understand anything."

Kaali merely nodded in agreement and took comfort in the rhythmic easing of Devi's pain.

Devi sighed and wished the girl would utter a word or two at least now and again. Female companionship at home would have been pleasant, even if it were a few words rather than she having to wander around the neighbourhood looking for conversation. It was a lonely existence having only sons, she would secretly have treasured a daughter to be at her side. The home would have had a more delicate touch, rather than the rough edges that all her sons had shown. Kaali, she admitted had made a huge difference to the cleanliness of the place, something all the lazy locals had not achieved, but at least they would happily gossip with her.

She thought back at her youth and her first pregnancy, there had been so much excitement and joy. With Kaali, it was more like waiting for death rather than a birth.

Abha sat in the car outside the chemist. He read through the doctor's letter then tore it up. He had no interest the future arrival of this misfortune. However, he took the prescription to the chemist as the last thing he wanted was her death or her child's dead body on his hands. Next door to the chemist was a hardware store with an array of cheap plastic and wooden items, mostly unwanted bargains. He spotted a wooden stool the same height as his front door step. They were common pieces in many an Indian kitchen. After some hesitation, he bought the stool and went back home to his wife and mother.

As usual, Kaali had her back to everyone as she stirred and chopped and engrossed herself in the preparation of the evening meal. Abha slammed down the bottle of medicine and addressed the table, "take a spoon of this every morning and every night."
He then carelessly put the wooden stool down in Kaali's corner.
"If you want to carry on behaving like a dog then sit on the floor, otherwise use this!"
Devi raised her eyebrows in astonishment, it was true it did not look good that the girl was always sitting in the corner on the floor when visitors popped through. Kaali too turned round slowly, looking down at the stool, but Abha had already shot out of the kitchen embarrassed that they would think that he even cared a jot. It was a pathetic, impulsive purchase but he was also getting irritated by her servile demeanour.

The boys trundled in except for Chetan and demolished the dinner, always teasing their mother who yelled at them threatening to beat them up with the broom. Kaali loved to listen to the laughter and jokes, she had never felt such warmth between family members, not even between her sisters, but never a smile passed her lips. She never showed signs of understanding or being part of the family other than to serve. She could not understand why she was unable to communicate and could only whisper or nod if a response was needed. The boys got used to her mannerisms and put it down to shyness and upbringing, but were mindful that their teasing did not make her too uncomfortable. They had an unspoken appreciation of this silent girl who never complained or smiled. They never directed any of their leg pulling towards Kaali when Abha was around, although Abha had made a habit of arriving late and eating dinner alone at the table while Kaali sat in her corner. He no longer felt free to express himself or laugh with his mother or brothers, Kaali had strangled his joy of living. Likewise, with breakfast, he would sit at the table when all the others had left for school or work. Weekends and holidays, he either ate before them or went straight out and ate in a street cafe. He found it hard to pretend that life was good with this heavy weight manacled round his ankles.

Chetan appeared late one evening after seeing a Hindi film, to find Kaali sitting on her stool in the corner waiting for Abha.

"You always wait up for my brother. He is a very lucky man."

Kaali, in denial of any compliment, took out the plate of food that had been kept aside for Chetan. "Why don't you ever smile? Are you not happy here? Ma can be a bit mean but she doesn't really mean it. I think she is very fond of you because you help her so much. We are all fond of you, you make all our lives so comfortable."

To his horror, Kaali found his kindness too much to bear and ran out of the kitchen to the bedroom. She sat on her blanket and buried her face in her hands trying to shut out his gentle words. If only he knew how unclean she was and how her brother had to suffer because of her, he would hate her too. She had no wish to express her feelings or utter the words to explain her innermost thoughts. She felt so ashamed and begged the gods to let her and the curse within her die at birth. She had heard many stories in her village where the medicine women would be unable to deliver a baby and both mother and baby would die. They would say that the women were being punished by the gods for their sins and no medicine could ever save them.

Kaali listened carefully to ensure that Chetan had left the kitchen before she ventured back and waited for her husband. She sat on her new stool, another act of kindness from her beloved husband, which she little deserved. She heard the car and quickly leapt up to get his food ready and boil water for the tea. She lay the table and stood waiting in her corner, ready to attend to his needs.

She stood, head bowed, swaying gently and waiting, then almost fell off balance as she nodded off to sleep. She realised that Abha had gone straight to the bedroom, he had not come to eat as usual. She had no idea what the time was or how long it had been since Abha had arrived. The tea and his dinner had all gone cold. Disappointed, she packed away the food and washed away the tea pot and mug. Creeping into the bedroom, she heard him snoring gently, so made her way to her bedding and rested her weary bones. She wondered what she had done to anger him that he had chosen not to eat the meal that she had prepared. It was the only big thing that she could do for him and she had failed.

CHAPTER 8

Kaali woke up to a quiet house. Abha was not in his bed. She hurriedly ran to the kitchen to find Devi sitting alone at the table drinking tea.
"Ah! So you get up when everyone has gone! With my poor legs I had to make breakfast and the tea. So you think just because you're going to have a baby, you can treat this place like a hotel. Take your medicine!! And go sit down on your stupid stool!"
Kaali was in shock. She thought she had just died and been sent back to earth by the devil to make others suffer some more.
Kaali started to clear the table when Devi yelled once again, "I said take your medicine first, child! Do you want to fall down dead on my kitchen floor! We pay all this money for a doctor and you treat it like a joke!"
Kaali now terrified that she had truly failed her

husband, quickly took a spoon of the sweet syrup which was sadly clearing the burning sensations. She missed the pain and the agony. She deserved to suffer and now she had overslept and not cooked his breakfast. She could not believe that she had not even heard Abha leave.

"When I was your age, I always woke up before my husband and made his breakfast. I never missed a day, not even when I was with child."

Devi walked out of the kitchen with a pronounced limp muttering about her lazy daughter-in-law who had not even oiled her legs that morning.

Kaali worked faster and harder than ever. She took out the rug from Devi's room and beat it and let the dust fly out. She washed the floors and walls out in the veranda. As she scrubbed, her mind calmed down and she wondered why she had not just been dragged out of her bedding instead of being left there.

Evening came too soon, Kaali washed her face in cold water to ensure that she never had a repeat of the previous night. As she sat waiting for Abha, she would wipe her eyes at intervals with a wet cloth, which she kept up her sleeve. She heard the car, sat patiently waiting for him to walk into the kitchen, once again he never came and went straight to the bedroom. She felt agitated that she had failed to make his breakfast and for two nights in a row he would not eat the dinner she had cooked.

She waited forlornly until she thought he had fallen asleep. She slipped into the room and glided like a snake to her bedding. She knew he was awake and held her breath listening to his heavy breathing. She wondered what she had done and what more she could do to serve him. She put the wet rag on her chest and curled on her side so that she did not have the comfort of too deep a sleep.

The next morning found Kaali up even before sunrise, perched on her stool, sipping her tea. Abha wandered in idly sitting on his mother's chair so that he had full view of the kitchen and any faces that passed by the barn door. Kaali leapt up to prepare his tea and breakfast, she had not expected anyone to rise so early and was angry with herself for not hearing his movements. She had slipped up many times recently and felt cross with herself for her incompetence.

Abha stared into space, always rummaging in his mind for solutions, only to find more problems. He sipped the hot, sweet tea and the aroma of frying onions tantalised his taste buds. In no time, the table had been laid with omelette, bread and hot chutneys.

Abha thought it was his right that she should dutifully serve and obey him. He was her master and had saved her from death in the village.

"You are not to sleep on the floor anymore. From tonight you sleep on the bed."

Kaali froze. Her growing stomach was causing more and more discomfort on the hard floor and she feared that she had disturbed him in his sleep and now he had offered to share his bed. How she would ever sleep again she did not know. Her pillow and her blanket were her comfort. She would lie and imagine the waters pressing down on her head. She could close her eyes and drown in the shame of her existence, always regretting waking up each morning knowing that she had not died.

She bent her head as submissively as was possible, knowing that she dared not disobey. The whole day, her mind was tormented by the night yet to come. Devi observed Kaali's preoccupation and wondered what was passing through her mind. After the rest of the rabble had eaten the food like jolly vultures and fled the nest, she started on her complaints.

"My legs are worse than ever, girl! You have to give them a proper massage today not the usual lazy hurried rub you give!"

Kaali got the warmed balm and sat on the floor, inwardly wincing with pain but outwardly calm and diligent.

"Bring the stool here to sit, you stupid girl. It's not glued to the corner, Abhu didn't get the stool for you just to sit on and drink tea!"

Kaali gratefully placed the stool next to Devi and began her gentle, but firm massage. Devi closed her eyes, basking in the immense comfort of the caring hands.

"Abhu is very busy with work these days. Always home late."

Kaali nodded but showed no other reaction.

"Since you came, he has to work so much more to feed you, buy you clothes, doctor's bills and now a baby on the way. You only came here with that dirty bundle. And throw that filthy blanket away. Even the rats wouldn't chew on that!"

Kaali stooped her head even lower to show her gratitude and the goodness that they had all shown towards her, but her mind was filled with the night yet to come.

The night was quiet and dark. She had just a small light in the kitchen and sat waiting clutching her shawl round her head and body. She waited and waited for the sound of the car. Her eyelids fought to shut but Kaali kept wiping them with her wet rag. Maybe he had already arrived and was in the bedroom, she must have fallen asleep and missed the noise. She tiptoed into the bedroom, but no sign of Abha. It occurred to her that maybe he wasn't coming home and that was why he had ordered her to sleep on the bed. She panicked that her very presence might have driven him her away and now that she was with child, it had disturbed him even more. She sat on the edge of the bed in despair, but again there was no way that he would leave his mother and brothers on the lurch.

Anil was unreliable and no longer cared about his wife or sons, he was a free agent who was answerable to no one. They all depended on Abha to be the rock and foundation of the family. The small clock at the side of his bed showed two in the morning. It now seemed very unlikely that he was coming home. But if he did come back and found her asleep in his bed instead of waiting for him to attend to his needs, she knew she would have failed him. Another thought crossed her mind that he may have had an accident and was lying by the roadside somewhere or in a hospital. Tears welled up knowing that she was useless in making any situation better.

Kaali went back to the kitchen and rocked herself on the stool, tears streaming down, anxious and frightened of the unknown, praying that no misfortune had befallen her husband.

So this was how Devi found the girl early in the

morning. She was curled on the floor, head down, still quietly sobbing and imploring God for forgiveness for all her sins. Devi could not bend nor stoop with her overweight frame and unbending knees.

"Get up, child. Didn't Abhu tell you he was away on business for a few days? Get up and go to sleep. There is nothing much to do. The boys won't be having breakfast at home today."

Devi waited while Kaali absorbed the words. She sighed with relief that her worst fears were unfounded, then crawled forward, kissed Devi's feet in gratitude and slowly lifted her weary body.

Her slim, dark face seemed ever more shrunken and skeletal. She pulled the veil well over her hair and face, struggling to walk forward, holding onto any piece of furniture or wall for support.

The complexities and demands of family life had toughened Devi over the years and it had been a long time since she had felt any compassion for another human being.

CHAPTER 9

No mention was made of this cursed day and Abha's name was not repeated either. Devi, not wanting to appear to have become soft-hearted, berated Kaali even more. Kaali attended to her mother-in-law and the needs of the household with no expression of pleasure or pain. It was rare that anyone spoke to her because they felt uncomfortable and were aware that any conversation made Kaali uncomfortable, so they all gradually withdrew any acknowledgement of her presence. A nod or shake of the head, or sometimes the utterance of a single syllable, was all that was needed.

Kaali slept on the bed each night dreading and longing for the day when Abha returned. When Devi peeped in now and again, all she saw was what appeared to be a shawl casually thrown into a heap in the corner of the bed. Even with her growing child, there was very little flesh on those scrawny bones.

After five days, Devi was eating her lunch and yelling at Kaali to sit and eat too.
"I keep telling you, stupid fool, if you don't eat, you and the baby will get sick. We can't be spending on doctors all the time because of your foolishness! You are not a child; why do I have keep telling you what to do! Everybody worries about you and you don't worry about anyone, not even your baby!"

The sound of the car engine outside, brought an abrupt halt to Devi's monotone. Kaali put her plate to a side and drew up her veil closer to her body. She leapt to her feet to put on the kettle and make tea for her husband.
"Ma!! How are your legs? I've had a very good business trip. I will tell you everything later but I'm too tired now. I need a good sleep after my tea. Even my back is hurting so bad after driving so much."
"Put some of this balm on. It's very good. My poor son, running around looking after everyone."
Abha took the bottle of tiger balm when Devi grabbed it back.
"The girl can do it, no point you trying to put this on your back. She is not doing anything else useful. Just sitting on her stool and drinking tea all the

time."

Abha paused for a moment then said quietly to Kaali, "Yes, and bring the tea to the bedroom too." Devi looked triumphant.

"Hurry up, girl! My son is working so hard. Take his tea and give his back a good rub! Take good care of him, he is looking after you so well! Why are you so ungrateful!"

Kaali followed Abha to the bedroom and placed his tea carefully at his bedside. With trembling hands she stood at his bedside waiting to ease his back pains. Abha loosened his belt, threw it on the floor and took off his shirt. He pulled down his trousers to just above his buttocks and lay on the bed face down and waited.

Kaali trembled as she leant forward to touch his body and gingerly knelt beside the bed. She rubbed her hands together with the balm before she placed her fingertips lightly just below his shoulders and made small circular motions. Tiny electrical currents passed through her body, the thrill and pain caused her to shudder. Her posture was uncomfortable with the swollen stomach preventing her getting too near the bed. Her focus was on the pleasure of her husband and not her own discomfort. Her body ached for his caress and approval. She felt his tense breathing ease and his muscles relax. She massaged his shoulders, neck and his whole back, up and down, waiting for a sign from him to tell her to stop. Her shoulders and arms ached. She dared not stop but slowed down her movements until finally he said flatly,

"Enough! Take my clothes, they all need washing. Have you been taking your medicine?"

Kaali nodded as she backed away and left the room.

She hurried through the kitchen to the backyard and washed her hands vigorously. Her mind was always confused as to how she wanted to be near Abha but subsequently felt dirty. She thought it was her shameful desires that made her unclean, not the touch of her husband who worked so hard to look after the whole family.

"There'll be no soap or water left by the time you finish!" Devi snarled through the back door when she heard the continuous splashing of water. "The tiger balm does not smell that bad! Ungrateful girl!"

Kaali leant against the wall not understanding the rights and wrongs of her own mind. She felt dirty then and she felt dirty now. She wanted to cleanse her mind and body but did not know how to get rid of the evil within her, the evil that had permeated into her soul. The desire that remained unfulfilled whenever she was near Abha.

Kaali's mind was in a confused state. There was anger, fear, excitement and joy. She did not know what trust was or what her purpose was in life. She had no self-belief and felt that her only salvation was to always serve others. Every desire for food or warmth was an evil to be conquered. Every thread of happiness in her warped mind had to be eradicated by suffering and self-loathing.

She plodded through the day with heavy heart, disgusted with herself for getting pleasure from massaging Abha's body. Hating the touch of his skin under her fingers and still finding a thrill of being allowed to touch. Even after washing her hands, she could still feel his body pressing against her palms as in the prickly bushes in another life.

The child inside her had also started to move to the farthest corner of her womb as if to prepare to resist against birth. Kaali's thoughts were for the moment and there was no preparation for the child either materially or otherwise.

She had memories of caring for her little sister, Indira, when she was born but had no idea how she had suddenly been delivered into this world. There was none of the excitement of knitting shawls or picking names. Life just happened and Kaali flowed through as if thrown into a black river and the currents carried her along, throwing her against rocks and branches.

Abha lay in bed dozing, soothed by the massage and running his mind through the events of the last few days. He was restless with life and had no wish to live his life like his father with over indulgence of food, wine and women and an almost permanent cigarette stuck in the side of his mouth. Kaali and the unborn was the result of a big mistake through no fault of his own other than having drunk too much and getting lost on the way. If she had not tantalised him by swaying her hips and looking at him with those innocent eyes of a young deer, he would not be in this mess.

But now, he felt that he was at a turning point in his life but his nightmare decision was what to do with the girl and her child. Living in this house was a strain and because of his mother, he had to let the girl sleep in his bed. But he vowed that after the child was born, he would throw her back on the floor with the child.

When night came, Abha ensured that he was the master of the bed and slept as if her presence at his side was a mere inconvenience. Kaali lay curled, shrinking her body, her breath shallow so as not too move a muscle. Even, the unborn, seemed to shrink and remain rigid within its womb.

CHAPTER 10

Days and nights passed uneventfully. Kaali's comfort was listening to Devi constantly berating her. Devi watched over the wretched girl, eager for new life to enter the household. The young sons brought vigour and energy into the evenings with their over imaginative tales, while Abha lived his secretive, parallel life where his scheming would be a turning point for all. Anil arrived home late each night, usually drunk and stomped straight to bed after first skulking around the kitchen leering at Kaali.

It was late one evening, when Devi watched as Kaali cleared the kitchen, shaking with every movement and fear in her eyes.
"Are you in pain, child?"
Kaali shook her head vigorously and continued to

scrub the worktop, at which point, Devi walked over with a surprising spring in her step and marched the girl back to her chair. Kaali quietly sobbed, the agonising intervals of pain throughout the day had frightened her as if death was at her door. She welcomed death but feared the hereafter.

Devi went to the neighbours and brought back two elderly women. They hurriedly lay towels, and sheets in the outhouse in the backyard and walked Kaali through with reassuring words. Devi put on the kettle and poured warm water into an old tin basin.
"By the time the doctor gets here, it'll be too late. These women will know what to do. Just do as you're told and everything will be alright."
Kaali lay on the stone floor, the agonising pain, the humiliation of her posture, she suppressed an outward scream with every wave of shock that electrified her body. Devi squatted on the floor, holding her hand and wiping her brow, uttering kind words that were alien to her. Devi feared that Kaali was too feeble to deliver this baby and felt a pang of guilt that she had allowed her to carry on doing all the household chores.
"Keep pushing, child, the baby will be out soon. Take deep breaths, it will help the pain."
Kaali followed instructions wondering what devil had possessed her that she should be in this

agonising plight. She felt as if her insides were being ripped out as the women started cackling excitedly. It was ten minutes before midnight, when I, Karishma, entered this world, unwanted and unwelcome, screaming for the comfort of the womb.

Devi and the women, after doing their best to tidy up and make mother and child as comfortable as possible, left us both to rest. Devi had wrapped the pathetic little creature that I was in an old towel and prompted Kaali to put me to her breast and left us both exhausted and disappointed.

Devi put her head round the door to the supposedly sleeping Abha and simply said "girl" and retired to her own room.

Kaali was back in the kitchen the next morning as if nothing out of the ordinary had happened. A shawl had been tied round her body and I was tucked inside as she had seen her mother do with Indira. Devi did not appear for breakfast. The boys ate fleetingly and dared not glance at Kaali. There was no mention of the baby. Kaali heard the car engine as Abha sped away.

Like a child with a broken doll, Kaali would regularly creep into the outhouse and feed and comfort my tiny body. A little shock of dark hair already shadowed my delicate face. There was no excitement or joy at my arrival but Kaali felt the deep responsibility that had been thrust upon her, the deep subconscious maternal instincts surfacing to protect and nurture me.

She went to the bedroom, made the bed and tidied up Abha's clothes. She then took her little bundle and pillow to the outhouse. She washed the bloodied sheets and hung them out to dry. The towels became a little crib to protect me from the cold, hard stone floor. Her aching body thrived on punishment and relentlessly she carried on with preparing the evening meal not knowing who would be home for dinner.

She longed to massage Devi's legs to show her gratitude and wandered if she should venture to her room and offer to do this. Kali took the bottle of balm and edged towards Devi's room to find it empty and quickly backed out in fear of being found in her room alone. Puzzled, she went back to the kitchen when she heard Abha's car. She disappeared into the outhouse and watched discreetly from the open doorway. There was no door or windows as it was previously used as an open kitchen until a 'modern' kitchen had been built attached to the house.

She heard Devi's voice in conversation with Abha as they entered the kitchen.

"Where are you, girl? What's happening about dinner?"

Kaali rushed forward and quickly started laying the table and preparing to serve the food into the dishes.

"My legs are so bad. The things I have to do for you! May God please keep me a place in heaven where someone will look after me." she wailed.

Mother and son ate their meal with Devi giving the latest information on the neighbours and Abha grunting acknowledgement at intervals. Kaali could also hear voices coming from the backyard near the outhouse. She worried that they would try to stop her sleeping there with the baby and inwardly panicked as to what she could do. She wished she could just run away but did not know where to go or how she would care for the baby unless she lived a life of begging and stealing. This would mean more shame on the family if she were caught.

Abha left the table only to be replaced by the rest of the young men who approached shyly as they knew of the events of the previous night. In fact, they were surprised that Kaali continued to do the cooking and chores as if nothing was amiss.

Chetan ventured to ask, "How is the baby?"

Kaali bowed her head graciously and gave a gentle

nod of assurance. Nothing more was mentioned about the baby. They ate and left without further ado.

"Have you fed the baby? Go and feed her now, what kind of a mother are you!" Devi shouted. Kaali went to the outhouse to find a mattress had been laid down with pillows, blankets and a curtain draped across the doorway on a pole. Tears of gratitude pricked her eyes as she sat to comfort and feed her baby.

I hardly cried. Not for milk and not for attention. I had been born into my mother's silent world where the aim was to occupy as little space as possible and punish myself for being born a girl. She would look at me with such tenderness and then blamed herself for loving me too much. She considered me her punishment for her evil deed.

Abha was my father biologically and nothing more. Kaali would place a finger gently to my lips, to silence me if she thought I was about to express myself or make a demand as any baby would. Devi, after the initial disappointment of having delivered a granddaughter was only too eager to hold the baby while Kaali massaged her legs or cooked and cleaned.
"The older I get, the harder life is, always having to

hold this baby or nothing gets done! And not even a boy!"

But despite her outward pomposity, she had grown a kind spot for my mother and me. She would stroke my cheek and tickle my tummy. The gentles tones were for my ears only.

Abha never looked at me or touched me even once. Anil would make loud jovial remarks but had no real interest in me. My uncles would have a little play with me as long as I was with Devi. Otherwise I was invisible. There were no momentous events such as my first tooth or my first steps. I just grew into my mother's shadow, knowing my place. She kept me clean and fed on the minimum requirements. There was only under indulgence and I was no rebel. Kaali would hold me close, wrapped in her shawl, sweeping the floor or chopping vegetables while she sat on her stool. As I grew, she would sit me on her stool while she maintained the steadfast care of the family.

CHAPTER 11

The home dynamics had altered with Abha staying away more nights on business. Anil also stayed away many nights but his whereabouts were never questioned. Ashok had moved to Kerala and was taking a more serious approach to catering and had found himself a position as a kitchen porter in a tourist hotel.

Chetan appeared to be falling in and out of love, earnestly seeking out a soul mate. His rickshaw lay discarded at the back of the house and he worked doing several casual jobs at the cinema and theatres. He too moved to Mumbai looking for bright lights and fame.

Devi was much more relaxed after reluctantly accepting that her elder sons were not going to become doctors, lawyers or rich businessmen. But deep within, she still wished that her two younger sons would have a more academic approach and make something of their lives.

Manish and Niraj had grown into more quiet steadfast teenagers, who felt that the responsibility for the household now belonged to them. Abha still provided sufficient income to look after everyone with money sent spasmodically by the absent brothers. It appeared that Manish and Niraj had developed an academic future. They poured over their books studiously and had aspirations to go to university much to Devi's delight. The quiet mysterious household had caused them to withdraw too, but never to ignore Devi or a light pinch of my scrawny cheek or pat on my head.

There were exciting days when the family would be together and have heated discussions over politics and forthcoming elections. There would be laughter and fireworks when India won the Test series against England. It was a very happy existence for my mother and me.

I was approaching my fourth birthday, sitting on the stool, playing with a wooden spoon and small pan. Devi had put in some dried pulses and leaves for my make believe kitchen. She occasionally slipped in some chocolate or sweets, as did my uncles. My mother was crouching next to me, sipping a cup of aromatic masala tea, every now and again stroking my hair. Then screams from Devi shattered the silence. We heard her hurling insults and shouting at Abha in the living room. Then Abha's imploring voice to reason and calm her seemed futile as she rambled on accusing him of all sorts of atrocities. She was pummelling Abha's chests with her fists.

My mother gathered me up and took me to our little home in the outhouse, our cosy little den, we huddled with closed ears waiting for the calm. One night, while I lay curled sleeping tight in my mother's arms, there were soft padded footsteps roaming outside our den. The heavy laboured breathing followed the shadow which crossed the curtain from side to side as the figure appeared to loom nearer than walk away, only to return once again. My mother pulled the blanket closer and snug around us, keeping her eyes on the swaggering shadow. A hand pulled a little chink in the curtain and Anil's blood shot eyes peered in. Kaali, petrified, frozen, numb with fear stared in horror at the frightening bearded face. It felt like a returning nightmare. Anil attempted to put on a drunken smile and placed a finger to his lips to silence her. But Kaali was already screaming inside her head and as he stepped into the den and placed a foot on the mattress. Kaali was vigorously shuddering and grabbed me, holding me so close that I feared my fragile bones would snap. I was violently dragged from my cosy slumber and screamed in pain and fear. My own piercing scream echoing my mother's terror, astonished Anil and he stood frozen, looking down at us angrily.

He stumbled out, only to be met by both Devi and Abha as he tried to sprint clumsily through the kitchen. The circumstance was only too obvious, although Anil made light of it and said that the child must be having nightmares. Abha said nothing and walked back to his bedroom. Devi looked through the curtain and found mother and child snuggled into the blanket, eyes tight shut and barely breathing. She too went back to her room acutely aware of the danger that lurked.

The next morning, the denial and cover up of the ugly incident was displayed by all the family members. The events of the previous evening had never happened. Anil was fussed over by Devi and praised for being the father of such an honourable family. The boys joined force to stamp out the seed of fear and doubt rather than admit to having a lecherous father. No one was willing to relinquish the family honour or bestow charitable thoughts on a lowly village girl who had wittingly penetrated herself into the heart of the Chettis' household. Devi even went to the front veranda to see her husband off to work, proudly standing between the white pillars for all to see. Anil, arrogant and insolent, swaggered off with no remorse but regret for an unsuccessful encounter.

Devi then followed Abha through to the living room to fuss over him and express her exaggerated concern that he had so many mouths to feed and so much responsibility. The voices were then lowered and a quiet, earnest conversation ensued followed by yells and angry screams from Devi. Once again the torrents of hysteria from Devi filled the house, injected with attempts by Abha to quieten her and still Devi cried hysterically. She was banging the sides of her head with her fists, while he tried to hold her and reason with her, his voice also rising to a crescendo.

As always, my mother scooped me up and took me to the outhouse, fearing that she was the cause of Devi's venom and displeasure. She closed my ears and held me close, breathing as one and waited patiently for the drama to be over.

The next few days were strained between the entire family. It was a house where the inhabitants walked on broken glass, wincing at every step. It had been a calm and pleasant existence when Abha and Anil were absent. Abha still never spoke to Kaali and only barked orders at her. He had no interest in my presence and ignored me completely.

However, Kaali's thoughts were now preoccupied with the terror of Anil's presence and was very mindful of being left alone with him. He would stare at her when she was alone in the kitchen, eyes boring right through her, desperate to dominate and exploit her. He had no fear of Devi or his sons knowing that any incident would be covered up to protect the family's honour. He had waited long enough and was consumed with a desire to possess her, if his son would not have her in his bed he would satisfy her, his depraved mind considered she would secretly be honoured by his attentions and passion.

Devi now stayed up late, sitting in the darkened lounge, ensuring that her errant husband did not wander in the wrong direction. Abha's tone towards Kaali was ever crueller and he snarled his displeasures, furious that she should now threaten to be the temptress of his father.

The remaining sons lived a silent existence, keeping out of the heightened sexual tensions between their father and brother. The fragile existence and relationship between the elders were too discomforting and they chose not to ask questions or intervene in matters that were none of their business. Within the family home they may as well have been deaf and blind so they mostly chose to spend their time at friends, libraries or tea shops. They were not as astute as their mother to truly understand what their brooding father was capable of.

It was on beautiful sunny day, with a pleasant breeze ruffling the curtains at the doorways, a day when the boys were out and Devi had wandered down the beaten track to visit a neighbour and elaborate on the successes of her sons. Kaali sat on the floor, sipping water while I played in our little outhouse, with my make believe family made of matchsticks. Anil marched into the kitchen, walked right past her towards me, which caused Kaali to leap up and trot after him. He laughed at her and spoke to me in a kindly voice, "Come little one, my first grandchild, I have got a present for you."
He took out of his pocket a small notebook and a packet of crayons. I followed his beckoning finger, I always obeyed like my mother. I followed him to the kitchen where he placed his gift on the small stool.
"Take your time and show me how clever you are. You must do a nice picture for grandad. I have to

talk to your mother now."

He turned and snapped his fingers at the terrified Kaali. She stood frozen, unwilling to succumb to his hideous threat of further mutilation.
"Back to your bed now or I will kill your daughter" he sniggered.
Kaali threw herself on the floor, sobbing, shaking her head from side to side, and beseeching for mercy, silently to let her be. Anil grabbed her by her ear and hair and dragged her to the outhouse. He was sober and had been watching the house, planning his move. I watched the drama and drew pictures of pretty houses in my new notebook. Like my mother, there was no automatic attack or defence mechanism. It was always submission. In fact, I was surprised to see my mother show any signs of protest and could not understand why she was not obeying the master of the household.

It was after a short time that my grandfather, stomped out of the kitchen, securing his belt as he went out. He did not even stop to look at my childish art which had been specially drawn for him. I could hear my mother washing herself outside and ran out to show her my picture: She looked smaller and darker than ever but nodded in approval of my masterpiece.

CHAPTER 12

Abha's only dealings with me so far had been to register my birth, Karishma Chetti, at Devi's request. Now here he was, telling Kaali that we both had to be ready to have our photographs taken. Kaali was in fear having no comprehension of what the future had in store for us and never having had a photograph taken. She had long been lectured about the sins of vanity and her own ugliness by her father and mother. She had rarely dared to look into a mirror and her reflection in a metal dish was always repulsive. She would look at me with wonder and cup my small impish face in her hands, amazed at the sweetness of my already chiselled bones. She never complimented me or voiced her love for me, but on this day she scrubbed my face and tied my hair back neatly into a long plait, mimicking hers and pinched my cheek as a sign of approval.

One of my rare car rides was always a joy and we sat patiently together in the back seat holding hands. The photographer was friendly and gave me a lollipop and gently prompted Kaali and me to pose for the photos while Abha waited outside the small cabin that served as a studio. He showed us the photographs for our approval and Kaali looked at our severe, startled expressions and shrugged her shoulders. Abha barged in and waved us aside, snatching the ugly images and pressed some bank notes into the photographer's hand.

We were returned to the house without further ado where Kaali was given forms to sign with no explanation. Abha was surprised at her neat handwriting and the care she took with the signature. Kaali could read well enough to see that these were passport applications but said nothing although she was now very curious. Leaving school at the age of twelve had been a huge disappointment for her as she had loved to study. She had already had a lifetime of experience at the age of sixteen but her talents had been muted into submission by her uncaring parents and now her unloving husband.

The next morning, Devi walked into the kitchen towards Kaali and held her momentarily stroking her hair, she wiped away a tear as she walked away.

Kaali, after being deprived of any physical show of affection for so long found this to be a shock to her broken body. She shuddered, knowing that Devi, in her own way had been kind to her and almost maternal. She clenched her fists, biting her lip, unwilling to surrender to her emotions and remained rigid with bowed head.

Devi went back to her room, stony faced, burying a sadness and regret within. The mood of the household remained in a sombre state for almost a month. There were many heated discussions between the brothers and visits from Ashok and Chetan. Anil was quietly observing my mother but did not speak. The four brothers formed a tight protective circle around Devi, always pampering to her moods and showing kindness in their response to any of her complaints. Abha was treated with new respect but there was also an element of suppressed anger towards him creating tension in their conversations.

My uncles showered me with new clothes and toys, much to my delight. They also bought little gifts for Kaali. But neither of us had any clue of what the future proposed. Kaali was unused to such attention, everyone would look at her directly to engage her in conversations and then smile and answer for her to relieve her of any awkwardness. They had finally begun to treat us, as if we were part of the family and Devi felt ashamed that we lived in the outhouse.

It was still early and Kaali was lying on her mattress, with me curled up next to her, willing herself to rise and start the day, when she heard movements already in the kitchen. Deftly, she entangled herself from my arms and floated into the kitchen. Devi was making tea. She could hear the boys talking quietly and Abha approaching. He gave Kaali a suitcase.
"Pack both of your things in this bag and get ready. We're going today."

Kaali, feared the worst that she was being rejected by her husband and was being sent away. If she had given birth to a son, life might have turned out differently. All the kindness offered by the family was simply sympathy and a form of farewell. She knew that if she were returned to her village our fate would be in the hands of her family who had also rejected her. But it was in her nature to obey and not to question. Her recent trauma had numbed her sensations but not enough that she was still not immune from pain and sadness. She had grown to love Devi and all her brothers in law and cherished her role in taking care of the family. Her feelings for Abha were far more complex, dominated by their first encounter where she had failed him.

I longed to remain under my cosy blanket but was carried through to be washed and dressed in new colourful clothes bought my uncles. She tied a ribbon at the top of my shiny plait then got herself ready in a sombre but smart salwar kameez. She then packed our clothes and items that had been gifted to us by my uncles. The bulk of the suitcase contained my clothes and toys. Devi walked in and placed a sari with blouse and underskirt in the suitcase, the very same ones that she had draped over Kaali many years ago, much to Kaali's astonishment. She then put two gold bangles on each of my Kaali's arms and a chain round her neck. She then gave her a pair of earrings in a box saying, "Get your ears pierced, I'm sorry I should have seen to it."

Kaali was confused. She still did not dare question anyone. She dropped to her knees to kiss Devi's feet, her only way of showing her gratitude and affection. But Devi kindly raised her by the shoulders and hugged her. She then hugged and kissed me, making me promise that I would always listen to my mother.

"Take care of Karishma, child" she said solemnly as she brushed a kiss on Kaali's forehead.

Chetan came to carry the suitcase through to the kitchen. We all ate breakfast together brought in by

the boys so that Kaali had no need to cook.
The atmosphere had lightened somewhat like in the old days when Kaali had first arrived. The younger brothers enjoyed some banter and teased me, making indirect affectionate remarks towards Kaali. Even Abha was in excellent spirits and joined in and Kaali could feel the energy and excitement vibrating through his body.

We were all then packed into a van with baggage ready for the journey. Chetan was driving, with Ashok squeezed in the middle between Chetan and Abha in the front seat. I sat in the middle row between Devi and Kaali. Manish and Niraj sat in the back with the luggage. It was a jolly group, with Kaali's silence an accepted part of the temporarily united family.

The drive seemed to take hours, with the brothers taking turns to drive. I happily slept on Devi's lap as she stroked my head and mumbled prayers totally oblivious to the jolly group of boys.

We arrived at the port of Madras with the boys somewhat more subdued. Each of them were trying to be more helpful than his sibling while constantly patting each other on the back as a gesture of reassurance. They unloaded the luggage while Kaali and I marvelled at the scene before us. There were throngs of people meandering in different directions. The noise was a constant roar of babble. The sun shone on the already sweaty bodies and well-oiled heads. Every face, whether happy or sad, showed purpose and destination. The parcels they carried and dragged came in all shapes and sizes. Some looked like nothing more than a large checkered or floral laundry bag tied up in string. The men's sarongs were as colourful as the women's saris. The local traders had mingled with the crowd, carrying their baskets of samosas and bottles of water. Every available space along the perimeter fence sat the cross legged street sellers with their jumping monkeys, toothbrushes and umbrellas. The gulls and the crows were competing for the crumbs and sometimes bold enough to swoop down and snatch a piece of bread before a hungry mouth was fed. The flies and mosquitos joined the party and feasted on the blood, sweat and tears of the unheeding crowd oblivious to their attackers.

Abha led the way while Chetan carried me through the throng. Devi took a tight hold of Kaali, linking arms while the remaining brothers followed. As we reached some large open gates, the cool breeze, carrying with it the salty sea air, reached our faces. It was exhilarating. The whole family gasped as before us opened up the vista of this huge iron ship gently rocking in the deep waters. There were many officials at various points and Abha stopped several times to ask the same questions. His nervousness was alien to him and however much he tried to appear calm and in control, his mind and words were gelling in confusion and excitement. Finally, a rather kindly but firm official, stated that beyond that point only passengers were allowed and directed the rest of the family to a viewpoint along a barrier where they could see the ship.

Devi broke into hysterical tears, wailing and grabbed hold of me. The brothers all hugged Abha, Kaali and me. Even Abha was in tears while he dragged me out of Devi's arms. I too cried desperately afraid of the ocean that lay before me and to see my mother sobbing with her hand held to her heart was too pitiful to see, even for a child of four. The luggage had been taken away and we walked the plank entering the mouth of the iron vessel that was to carry us into another world. We walked along the deck, the three of us still crying, squeezed into a gap to look for Devi and my uncles. It was an unusual sight and a strange feeling. This was the first time Abha had ever carried me or comforted me. I felt that my status and existence in the world had elevated to the highest degree. Additionally, he had his arm around Kaali, holding her close to ensure that she did not get lost in the crowd and maybe trying to protect her from her sadness. We looked like any other close knit happy family who were going on holiday. I would have boarded this ship many times over just to feel this sense of love and belonging. Kaali too rested her head lightly on Abha's chest as he held her, feeling calmer and not wanting to move.

Abha called out, "Look, there's your grandma and uncles. Can you see them waving...? "

We all waved wildly loosening our grip on each other. Devi was waving her handkerchief, stopping at intervals to dry her eyes.

This hot summer's day in August 1962 transformed our lives forever.

CHAPTER 13

The ship gently rocked in the lulling waves as the captain shouted out orders to the passengers and crew. The orders were relayed over the loudspeakers in Tamil, Hindu and English. The ship was moving away from the port and the screams from the shore and the passengers were getting louder and more desperate. The engines crunched and roared. Chains clanged as anchors were pulled up. The deafening noises ripped out the sadness of the parting and the passengers began to excitedly move around to get better views of the magnificent sea. The crowds on the shore disappeared from sight until all that was left was a thin line on the horizon. The passengers started to mull around looking for their cabins and their belongings.

Abha had cards with our cabin number and we

proceeded to walk the gangways in search of our temporary home. He had by now put me down but still kept a tight hold of my hand while Kaali followed close behind. Abha constantly voiced his thoughts on the mission in front of us to work out how to find our cabin. His own personal engine was running high on an adrenalin infused excitement.

We climbed down to a lower deck and eventually entered a small cabin where our bags had been placed. The cabin was furnished with a single bed and a bunk bed. There was a chest of drawers, wardrobe with attached dressing table and a mirror. A tiny ensuite bathroom, clean and white, was such a joyous luxury for us. There was even a hint of a smile on Kaali's lips. Abha was still chattering away both excited and also conscious of the new intimacy which made him nervous.

He unlocked the suitcases and Kaali unpacked his clothes, lovingly placing them in the drawers. She was calm and beamed with pride that her husband should have strived and achieved such a goal. She suppressed her joy and excitement with her habitual feelings of unworthiness. She had momentary lapses where she would look through the porthole and see herself falling down into the depths of the sea and her eyes would close over the welcoming end. She would free Abha from the burden of caring for her.

In her dreams she would take me with her but in reality she knew that she was too much a coward to take her own life let alone her daughter.

We walked back to the upper deck and made our way to the restaurant. Kaali and I had never expressed our hunger before and until Abha proclaimed that we should go and eat, we had remained silently berating our stomachs for wanting food. Again sitting at a table at close proximity, together, was alien to us. It was awkward. There was no conversation. Abha talked about everything and nothing attempting to cover up his nervousness. Kaali nodded to acknowledge that she was paying attention. Her conversations remained internal. She wanted to speak but it would take time for the years of silence to thaw out.

I did not feel nervous or awkward but in awe and fascinated by this whole new world. I was a child and this was an unbelievable and amazing adventure. After dinner, Abha took us back to the cabin giving landmarks to Kaali so that she would start to find her way about. Kaali already knew her way but never showed her ability or chose to outshine Abha in any way. He went back to socialise, at the bar, much to our relief. We had all been suffocated with our day of unnatural family bonding.

My mother lay down on the lower bunk and held me close. Tears pricked her eyes. Tears of a confused happiness of a strange new life and memories of a previous dark life. I was exhausted and pressed close into her bosom and fell asleep. She was in danger of falling asleep too and after gently settling me down, went into the bathroom to test the waters. She submerged herself in the glorious warm bath, still in her underskirt and blouse. She could never be naked even for a single moment. She dared not linger for too long, lest Abha returned and dressed into an old salwar kameez for bed, with a towel wrapped round her thick, wet locks.

Kaali laid out Abha's sarong on the bed and put on the bedside lamp beside it. She crept back beside me and lay wait for her husband's return, not sure what to expect but using me as her shield. She lay motionless, eyes closed, willing the return of Abha, yearning for his touch and drowning in her own self-disgust. The door opened, quietly. She felt his eyes upon her form and his fingers just barely brushed her hair. She could smell the sickly sweet breath as she had many years before, a reminder of the dark past. Then the spell was disappointingly broken and he busied himself in the bathroom before sliding under the blankets of his own bed. She knew he lay awake and only closed her mind when he succumbed to sleep.

The days and nights passed by, each night more electrifying than the previous. We established a routine where after breakfast, my mother would take me to the nursery where I played happily alongside other children and the impressive toys. I still hardly spoke and never cried but had started to utter a word or two in my attempts to express my pleasure. Kaali would sit in a corner watching and had taken to reading the children's books from the library. They were in the main Indian languages including English. Her casual gaze did not give away her intensity of concentration and her desire to learn. Lunch was always a casual buffet meal where we generally did not see Abha. The main evening meal was always together as a family. Abha was now more relaxed and confident, speaking freely. He often pressed Kaali for a response and she would oblige with a half-smile and gentle nodding of her head.

Sometimes the three of us would stroll along the deck together, Kaali and I always a couple of paces behind, marvelling at the magnificence of the sea and breathing in the cool salty air. The days were marvellous but lingering in the background was always the looming night with its dark desires.

One morning after such a restless night by all, with stormy seas and howling winds, Abha proclaimed that from that night onwards the child was to sleep on the top bunk. The rest of the day shrunk and time would not stand still. I could not bear the thought of not sleeping next to my mother who had been at my side since birth and Kaali felt vulnerable for having desires and berating herself for being a wanton human being.

Finally, the dreaded curtain of darkness fell and I could no longer keep my eyes open and fell asleep in my mother's arms as we sat in the cold breeze out on the deck. Abha carried me back to the cabin with Kaali dragging her weighted limbs behind. I was delicately placed on the upper bunk and swaddled in a blanket in an utmost paternal manner, with my mother also fussing around the bedding as if it could never be comforting enough.

No longer able to busy herself, she slid into the lower bunk with lowered eyelids and uplifted heart. Abha waited patiently and nudged Kaali into the farthest side and slid in next to her. So after nearly almost five years their marriage was finally consummated, she with dread and longing and he with kindness, desire and a boyish clumsiness. The nightly visitation to satisfy his needs gave Abha a masterful purpose in this new relationship, disappearing afterwards to the deck or bar or wherever the swaying ship took him.

Kaali would numb any sensations, limp in the arms of her husband and then immerse herself in her nightly ablutions, scrubbing and cleansing herself of the unwelcome joy and happiness that was her sin.

It was almost three weeks that the epic voyage lasted. Kaali had made no friends and all those who had attempted to connect had given up bored of her servility and lack of conversation. I had become more vocal and was always overjoyed when any child chose me as their playmate for the day. Abha had struck many liaisons at the bar with exchanged addresses and promises of supporting each other once their new life began in England.

It was our last evening meal together and Abha talked, excited and agitated, stating that Kaali must start answering people or she would look a fool and make him look a fool. He would have to find a job and she would have to manage taking me to school and doing the shopping amongst other chores. He would have preferred to come alone to establish himself, except for his mother's fury and fear that he would desert both wife and child and never come back. He spoke crossly when he thought of the cutting remarks of his mother who had never spoken harshly to him before. He stressed the additional burden and pressure he was under and would have been much easier if he had come alone. He declared that his dream was always to come to England and have a prosperous life for himself and his family. It had never been in his plans to marry so early in life to a poor girl but he was doing his duty and looking after her. She was to understand how lucky she was coming from nothing and now about to start a new life in England because of him. He looked into her eyes, unblinking and said that if he had not married her she would have been stoned to death or drowned by her father. He was her saviour. His actions that had triggered the sequence of events were no longer an issue. He remained blameless and the honourable victim. Kaali bowed her head low to the table, unable to eat any more. Her pathetic view on life caused her to see her circumstances in exactly the way that Abha had described. She had shamed her family and Abha had saved her, unworthy as she was. Now she was going to start a new life in a strange country but her only desire was to serve Abha.

She was his property and his grateful slave. She would obey him, care for him unflinchingly and pray that she would bear him sons.

CHAPTER 14

We landed in England on 1st September 1962.
The sky was grey and there was a deep chill in the morning air. Everyone seemed to be dressed in shades of black, grey or dark blue. The faces were pale and unsmiling, everyone intense with purpose.

The language was peculiar to my ears and I strained to understand the garble that surrounded me. Kaali's drooping demeanour suited the grey landscape. It made her even more invisible as if she was destined to live in the mist and fog forever. Abha was busy negotiating with his new found friends as to the next move and before long we found ourselves and our luggage in a shiny black cab, the cleanest I had ever seen.

We arrived at a place called World's End which

frightened me as to what lay beyond. We were all in a daze and not really taking in detail the events of the journey until we climbed out of the smart black cab. We were directed by Abha to stand by some black railings with the luggage. Abha walked up and down the strange road where all the buildings looked exactly the same, holding a piece of paper with an address. He then climbed down steps to a door at the basement and knocked cautiously and we heard his stuttering conversation.

After sometime, he reappeared smiling broadly like an excited, young boy who had found treasure. He ushered us both down the steps and between us, we carried the luggage and followed him down to the basement flat. I was shivering with the inadequate layers of clothing and Kaali held me close while a pink faced, grey moustached elderly man chattered to us very amiably.

He took us on a guided tour of the flat. The kitchen was strange and alien to what we had been previously been used to. There was very little floor space covered with a black and white chequered linoleum. A cooker with electric rings, two cream cupboards with worktop and shelves on one wall were the furnishings. A large, deep, enamel sink cracked at the edges, faced the basement window on to a brick wall. The farthest door through the kitchen, led to the toilet, grey and cracked with a rusted chain. The living room with its heavily patterned wallpaper, beige with dark brown leafy prints, looked more inviting. A carpet with similar but harshly clashing pattern covered the small room. The bare mantelpiece craved delicate ornaments to offer some form of comfort and homeliness. An electric bar heater sat cold and dusty. The sparsely furnished room still managed to look overcrowded and cluttered with its shabby and dingy contents.

There were two tortuous bedrooms, one with an old double bed, chest of drawers and sink and a second small room which was tightly packed with a single bed and no space for anything else. We understood nothing of what lay before us. How we should cook, how we should eat, how we should bathe and how we should keep warm.

Mr Aidan Jones shook hands with Abha and asked him not to hesitate to contact him if we needed any advice. He had already directed Abha to the nearest local shops to buy provisions such as bread, milk and coal. He seemed a kindly man and offered to bring back some spare blankets and a saucepan which we could use until we had managed to get organised. After he left, Abha said that he would go to the shops and get the basics so that we could at least eat and keep warm.

I sat with my mother on the single bed, entwined in her arms, cold and hungry. It was getting dark and we dare not even switch on a light.

Eventually, Abha returned after what seemed like hours, Mr Jones returned with him and they arrived with a kettle, blankets, bread, milk, tea and other basic provisions. The lights were turned on and Abha was shown the coin meter for our electricity supply and warned us that the heater would drain the supply very quickly and we should always ensure that we had enough coins. He once again left us with a quick nod of his head in our direction and pity in his eyes.

Abha set to work straight away, putting on the kettle and making tea, much to Kaali's shame and embarrassment. But the warm sweet tea tasted good, just holding the cup in our freezing hands was a comfort. We feasted on pilchard sandwiches, never had bread been so white and soft and after tentatively using the toilet and washing in freezing water, we all snuggled into the same double bed to keep warm. It was a lasting, restful, deep sleep, preparing us for the unkind future.

CHAPTER 15

The days passed into weeks where every new experience became a learning, tolerance and acceptance game. This was a game at which my mother excelled. She would bend and sway whichever way the wind blew, never a complaint and so much humility.

She learnt how to cook a thrifty but tasty meal with rice, lentils and the poorest cuts from any meats, which were only served to Abha. She handled the notes and coins with care, accounting for every penny that Abha would reluctantly hand over to her. She observed roads, landmarks and took me to school and knew the cheapest markets to do any shopping. The rain, fog and the cold winds were her friends. Her language skills improved but still she was not a conversationalist as such, at least not with her husband. She read notices on my school boards, bus stops or at shop windows, always searching for something to protect us and improve our lives. She never put on the electric heater if she was alone in the flat.

She joined the local library and we would visit it most days after school where we kept warm and read the adventures of fairies and elves.

Abha had got a job in a warehouse, but the physical strain was not something that he was used to. It deeply depressed him that he could not get a job in an office and have a successful business.

He would occasionally bring home beer bottles which were upgraded to whiskey on pay day. The excitable optimism he had on the ship gradually faded. He became surly, bitter and complained that he was held back from success because his mother had forbidden him to leave us behind. Once again he bemoaned the fact that Kaali was the cause of all his bad luck and I was now an additional burden. He boasted of his abilities and how there would be a day when his work colleagues would pay him more respect.

He had no interest in what Kaali did each day or how I was coping with my new school. After all the initial registrations and form fillings and strutting about arrogantly with his briefcase, he had an expectation of being somebody of importance, but instead he felt that his future had been strangled by our very existence.

He failed to see that Kaali was becoming wiser to self-reliance. He failed to see that my academic abilities were higher than my counterparts and mother and daughter were forming an intellectual bond, far superior to the emotional one that had held us together for so long. He failed to see the stirrings of my sibling who would venture into our world, not knowing if it would be wanted. I had been taken under the wing of a classmate called Carol. She would proudly take charge of my needs and ensure that no one laughed at me because of my poor clothes or lack of language. Her mother, Joan was one of the dinner ladies at my school and would gently approach Kaali to guide her and give advice. Kaali trusted Joan and sometimes asked her to explain a school letter or similar.

One day, Abha opened his eyes astounded when Kaali quietly told him that she had got a job at my school as a dinner lady. To have managed to get a job, earn money in her own right without even asking his permission was an insult. He was thankful that, at least in his eyes, it was a menial job. He questioned the salary and the hours. Kaali gave him all the details openly and honestly. He was not a fool to appreciate the advantage and immediately declared that it should be more than enough to buy food and clothes for herself and the child and he would not be giving her any more money. Kaali meekly nodded but relished the thought that she could spare Abha from some of the responsibility and burden.

But all was not in vain, items began to appear in the basement flat which was Abha's way of feeling like a successful man. A rented television appeared one day, followed by a paraffin heater which was far cheaper than the electric fire. It became Kaali's duty to go regularly to the petrol station and fill up the paraffin gallons. This was followed by a tin bath and large pan so that Kaali could boil water for our weekly baths. The paraffin heater often doubled up as a stove where a soup simmered away or water was left to heat for the baths.

Before Abha came home, my mother and I would sit in front of the television watching cartoons while we ate hot buttered toast and drank sweet tea. She would disappear into the kitchen before he returned and I would follow her or creep into bed with a book.

The days that followed were not unpleasant, we kept out of Abha's way in the evening when he sat in front of the television, drank moderately, but enough to loosen his tongue to hurl insults and blame in our direction. We would cautiously edge into the second bedroom where we now slept.

Library books were laid orderly under the bed. We read and whispered by the dim light until we fell asleep.

CHAPTER 16

Kaali could feel the familiar stirrings of life inside her womb. She looked at Joan beseechingly and gently stroked her stomach.

"My dear, you have a bun in the oven! Have you been to the doctor?"

Kaali shook her head with a sigh.

"Don't worry love, we'll make an appointment and go together after work. I bet you haven't told your husband yet either!"

Joan suspected that all was not normal in the Chetti household and whether it was the culture or her husband was just another male chauvinist was of no interest to her. She felt duty bound to help this gentle creature who seemed so alone and always so sad.

I also relaxed in Carol's company and learnt to play like a true child and was in awe of her soft curly fair hair. She would call me Kari unable to get her tongue round the unfamiliar Karishma. We would link arms and stroll around the playground while Carol whispered harmless secrets about the other children and teachers. I would return the favour by helping Carol with her maths and written work. I had an exceptional neat hand and could perform acrobats with figures in advance of my age. I felt it was my upbringing that helped me to simply absorb, follow and copy without question. Learning was never a chore and my mind welcomed knowledge of every kind.

The following day the four of us strolled together to the surgery. Carol and I walked in front holding hands and Joan and Kaali followed close behind. Joan constantly chattered about anything and everything, her pregnancies, her husband, her constant diets and the weather. Kaali listened with great interest, the only glimpse she really had of how others lived their lives. Leaving us in the waiting room, Joan went into the surgery with Kaali at her request.

Dr Flanagan was efficient and business like. Her questions were professional, her examination of Kaali clinical and her listening skills were non-existent.

"She was a bit rubbish wasn't she!" exclaimed Joan on the way home in such a tone that it even made Kaali bring out a twisted grin.

"Well at least we know that everything's alright. And don't worry, love, I'll come with you to the antenatal clinics. But you'd better tell your hubby that there's another one on the way!"

They parted at the corner and each went back with their child to their respective homes. Kaali knew that there would be no comfort in saying anything to Abha. The sequence of events would have to flow in the way that the Gods wished. Security, peace and happiness were alien to her and she had no expectations for herself or the coming birth.

Abha arrived home earlier than usual in a foul mood. He had been fired. He caught Kaali and me sitting cosily together watching TV and drinking tea. It inflamed his mood even more and lunged at us with clenched fist. Kali instinctively darted between me and the devil, pushing me towards to the door and received the full force of his thrust. The hot tea spilt over his trousers and Kaali landed on the floor. He kicked her aside ranted about the treatment he had received from his employer. The true version of events was that he was far too busy looking important than actually doing any work.

Kaali limped to the kitchen to make tea and food for her husband, disappearing into the bedroom momentarily to bring him a clean sarong so that she could wash his tea stained trousers.

He complained about the tea, the food and now the issue of income. He had been given one week's pay and asked to leave the premises immediately. Abha did not fear that he would be without a job; his complaint was that he had been made to feel inferior and useless. He would show them that there were better opportunities for him than what they offered.

Kaali remained in the kitchen, cleaning up after the meal, bringing a bowl of food to the bedroom for me and washing Abha's trousers and other clothes. She took the tray from his lap when he called and served his every need as any obedient servant would. He called for his briefcase, pen and paper and went through his notebook of all the contacts he had made on the ship and his various travels around India. He watched TV and drank his beer. He noticed a newspaper wedged in the corner of the sofa.

"What the hell is this? Did you buy this? You have money to buy a newspaper and watch TV and sit around drinking tea? And since when did you start reading, maybe you're the new Mayor of London!"

He rolled up the newspaper and started to whack Kaali to drive her out of the room and back into the kitchen.

"You are an ugly fool and have no appreciation of what I have to put up with because of you!"

He sat back in his chair opening up the newspaper and browsing the contents, continually grunting and swearing under his breath. Kaali sat on the kitchen floor, regaining her breath and holding her stomach. If only she could find a way to get rid of this thing growing in her stomach, instinctively she knew that it would only add to the pains of her already fragile existence.

CHAPTER 17

The peace and harmony which Kaali and I had had during the day disappeared with Abha constantly nipping at our heels and barking orders. It was a huge relief to leave the flat and go to school. Kaali could no longer go to the library, but had to return to make breakfast and tea for Abha. She would boil water for his bath and he even got her to shave him each day, he was spiteful and like his mother ensured that she never remained idle. By mid-morning he was ready to venture out smartly dressed, carrying his briefcase, to look for employment and Kaali would go back to school to carry out her dinner lady duties.

She loved her job and all the happy smiling faces of the children. She had a sense of pride to see me in line and I could sense the joy that all the pain in the world could not erase.

Kaali refused offers from Joan to bring me home after school, for to collect me was her show of devotion and an escape from the flat as now Abha would return at any time of day.

The weather was gradually changing, we would see some welcome sunshine and the days were getting longer. It seemed like therapy for all the people with playground chatter getting louder, parents congregating in huddles and lingering for a chat, their austere attire transformed into lighter, brighter clothing. The trees were sprouting leaves and buds and the excited birds flitted about looking for a suitor and a cosy place to nest. The world outside was uplifting but our basement flat was shielded from the sunshine of the coming spring.

However, Abha was in better spirits after securing a job at the Indian Tea Centre. He liked his smart uniform unlike the work overalls of his last employer. He felt elevated that he was trained to use the cashier's till and enjoyed banter with the customers. His effervescing charm completely hid the unkind, callous man beneath. But at least it meant that Kaali and I had our days back again where we could spend time in the library or just go window shopping. Occasionally, Joan would tell us about a jumble sale at a local church or school and we would all go together. We had fun rummaging through the rows of tables with clothes, shoes and other unwanted items. Kaali was obviously very careful with her limited resources.

One Saturday, Abha was at work and Kaali and I had gone to a jumble sale with Joan and Carol at the local church. At a bric-a-brac table, Kaali spotted a figurine, mottled black and grey marble about eight inches in height. She stroked the smooth, robed statue, turning it round and round in her hands. There was a chip at the base of the neck and one of the toes was missing.
"Do you like that?" asked Joan surprised. "It's a bit morbid don't you think?"
"I like it," smiled Kaali.
The rotund woman behind the table spoke up, "I think it's a Hindu god, I'm not sure, I don't even know where we got it from. Do you want it?"
The contents of Kaali's purse were limited as she took a peek. The woman took the statue and wrapped it in newspaper and handed it to Kaali. "Go on. Take it. Looks like it means something to you. Nobody else is going to want it."
Kaali smiled gratefully, "thank you very much".
Joan too smiled her appreciation at the woman, "bless you, dear. You've made my friend very happy."

Kaali took home the Goddess of Time and Death, wrapped it carefully with a clean piece of cloth and lay it gently under her pillow.

Days and nights followed with a routine of joy, despair and anxiety. Abha came home each day relating events with illusions of his empathy with customers. All the regulars knew him as the cheerful chappie and the management noted his ability to charm and bring back the customers. He was rewarded by being called into the manager's office, commended and given a pay rise. The elation of being recognised was bubbling like a bottle of champagne ready to pop. He picked up some beer and whisky on the way home, eager to expound to his spouse the splendour of his achievements.

He walked into darkness. It was a shock. Kaali would always be there to take his coat and fuss over him and listen to his every word. He called out as he checked the bedrooms.
"Where are you, woman! Where the hell are you?"
There was no food to eat. The flat was cold where she had failed to light the paraffin heater before his arrival. The woman and the child were nowhere. He sat down dumbfounded.

There was a gentle knock on the door. It was Joan. Behind her stood Carol and myself.

"I'm sorry I couldn't come sooner, but your wife is in hospital and the baby is on the way."

Abha looked on uncomprehending and confused.

"Don't worry," carried on Joan, "I'll keep Kari at my place and take her to school tomorrow, if that's okay with you."

Abha nodded, still in shock.

"I've written down the hospital details for you, it's only a fifteen-minute walk luckily. Also, the hospital gave this list of things you need for the baby when it comes home."

Abha thanked her suspiciously and closed the door. He made no eye contact with me but could see Carol and me with linked arms.

Abha sat back in his chair in darkness taking it all in. Kaali was having a baby in hospital, result of his weakness and kindness on the ship. But strangely more profound was that how Kaali had managed to befriend an English woman who would even keep the child while she was in hospital. The first thing he had to do was to forbid this friendship as he did not want Kaali to be influenced or have any aspirations of any other way of being. He knew this was a result of her job as a dinner lady and that too must stop. He had heard from colleagues that some of the wives worked as home machinists to earn extra money. This would ensure that Kaali did not leave the house in future.

The immediate problem was that Kaali was in hospital. He looked at the piece of paper and knew exactly where the hospital was. But he was hungry and thirsty. He gulped down a beer and made his way to a local curry shop where he feasted, celebrating his success alone. Outside, he pulled out a couple of cans of beer from his pockets and downed these too.

He finally arrived at the hospital and after making enquiries at reception found his way to Kaali's bedside. She lay there slight and exhausted, eyelids lowered as always and whispered, "Boy" pointing at the cot beside her.

Abha walked over to the cot and lying there swaddled lay the tiny form of his baby son. He lifted him up gently and muttering his thanks to God and kissing him on the forehead lay him back down with tears in his eyes. He rejoiced that he had a son, not suspecting for even one moment that in fact his son may have been his brother.

Abha went to a phone booth where he could use his cheap rate phone card, for one of his infrequent calls to his mother. He gaily chattered to Devi about the birth of his son, his successes at work and his enviable new life. Devi was ecstatic.

"My dear Abhu, I have prayed every day to Lakshmi for your prosperity and happiness. I must go to the Temple and find a good name for my first grandson. You are a good son and sending me postal orders, may God bless you always. Your father can't work anymore. The doctor says he has problems with his liver and too much sugar in his blood. Your brothers are doing their best but you know what medical bills are like!"

She whined on in her sing song manner about her ailments and the local gossip until finally the money on the card ran out much to Abha's relief.

CHAPTER 18

Devi was insistent that the new arrival should begin with the letter 'A' like her husband and eldest son. The temple chose the name Amitabh and so the new addition began life carried in his father's arms to his home. Kaali followed behind in a semi glow of contentment, wincing at every step with the pain of post birth trauma. Abha had gone through the hospital list and already bought a few clothes, nappies and a shawl to bring the baby home in. All this was alien to him as back home his father and uncles never concerned themselves with these things and left it to the women as part of the domestic duties.

Abha had a strange sense of fulfilment in providing for his son. He would stroke his cheeks every morning before he went out to work and every evening when he came home, "Amitu, my little baby. You're going to be a big strong boy like your daddy." Or "you're going to be a clever boy like your daddy."

The home front was also firmly reined in to follow his rules. Kaali was forbidden to socialise or work outside the home. A company visited with a sewing machine, training Kaali to sew parts of garments and offered Abha a fixed amount for every fifty pieces sewn correctly. They returned weekly and collected the pieces and paid Abha.

Kaali was busy with the new baby, school runs, sewing and administering to Abha's needs. Joan had backed off when Kaali had looked at her sadly and walked away. She knew that the husband was the domineering sort. She had been surprised that when she had knocked on the door when Kaali had been admitted to hospital, that he had not even glanced or spoken to me.

She ran after Kaali and whispered, "It's alright, I understand. But if ever you want any help you can always count on me."
Kaali listened and walked on.
Amit or Amitu, as affectionately called by Abha, was always crying with a runny or blocked nose and not settling to any sleep pattern. Kaali and I were

constantly tired with lack of sleep. We three were now in the larger bedroom while Abha slept peacefully alone in the single room with the door firmly shut. In the mornings, my brother would be harnessed round Kaali's chest while she prepared breakfast and boiled water to wash. I was now five approaching six, but already wise beyond my years. I would rock my brother while Kaali hurriedly prepared a meal or kept Abha's clothes ready for his return home from work. During the day, every moment that Amit slept, Kaali would be at the sewing machine, churning out each piece carefully and methodically. There was no payment for any piece that was not perfection. She had learned from her mistakes and the slaps for her carelessness. We had no time to read together or go to the library. I missed the moments where we sipped sweet tea in front of the television.

I loved when my mother combed my hair each morning. She would rub a little oil into her fingers and run them through my hair, easing out the knots and smoothing out any rogue strands. She would comb it all back and then run her fingers along the top of my head to the nape of my neck, separating into a severe clean path. Each half then became a stiff plait like snakes entwined unwillingly and secured by a rubber band. Each plait hung just above my waist. I dearly wanted a ribbon and bow like Carol. I knew there were some given by my grandmother and uncles, but they remained unpacked in the suitcase under our bed. I did not dare to unbalance my mother's fragile mind with even a simple request for a ribbon.

Amit was not an easy baby. He cried constantly and demanded attention at all hours. It delighted Abha to see Kaali struggling to cope with the crying baby and taunted her saying, "you don't even know how to look after my son. My mother looked after the girl and see she never cried!"
In the very same breath he would add "what rubbish have you cooked for my dinner! How am I supposed to eat this!"

The additional problem was that now Kaali was forbidden to handle money. Abha would bring home a few provisions on his way home from work. He did not ask what was needed and she did not dare to tell him. If they were running short of anything, she would leave out the almost empty packet hoping that he would register this. If tea was running low, she would not have any until a new packet was brought home. It was a miracle that she did not die of hunger and starvation.

Kaali was growing physically weaker daily. Lack of sleep, lack of food and the constant strain that she lived under was taking its toll. I was fortunate that I escaped to school each day and was given the daily ration of milk and a hot meal at lunchtime. Carol would always bring two bars of chocolate biscuits which she would share with me at break times. Joan's attempts to converse with Kaali were futile but she feared for the obvious fragility of her friend. She was previously a dark shadow that glided past but now she was the whisper of death. If you had seen her asleep, you would have thought that she was dead.

Kaali often caressed her little statue and held it close to her breast. She felt unworthy of everyone who crossed her path and knew she had disappointed them in some way. She begged for forgiveness for wanting her unborn child dead and thanked God for the blessing of her son. She pleaded with God to give both her children a life of love and peace. She offered her own life as sacrifice. She prayed for health and prosperity for her husband and also Devi who had shown her so much kindness. She begged for forgiveness for all her sins, the biggest sins which still lay within, tainting her body daily. Then lovingly she would put her little goddess under her pillow before she closed her eyes hoping to catch at least a fragment of sleep.

CHAPTER 19

It was a normal evening where Abha sat in front of the television, drinking beer and cursing Kaali for any trivial reason.

Kaali was in the kitchen washing the pots and dishes with the snivelling baby harnessed to her chest. I no longer played or read at home and was folding the dry laundry.

A loud knock at the door quietened Abha, Kaali and I exchanged glances not knowing who it could be. It was not the day for the sewing company to collect the pieces and nobody else was expected.
Abha, in his sarong and T-shirt peered through the net curtains and saw a well-dressed man and woman, not anybody he recognised.
He opened the door a fraction, "Can I help?"

"Good evening, my name is John Barrett and this is my colleague, Susan Johnstone. We're from social services and we've just come to have a chat."
They produced ID cards and made their way in before Abha could remonstrate.
"Sorry to come at this hour, but we did want to catch the whole family at home."
Abha looked at them suspiciously and felt at a disadvantage, wearing a sarong and not looking as professional as his visitors.
"It's just that since the birth of your child, we have no visits from your wife to the clinics for postnatal check-ups, immunisation or general weigh-ins for the baby. We just want to make sure everyone is in good health."

While John Barrett spoke, Susan looked around the living room and noted the clean, tidy environment and on the surface there was nothing out of the ordinary.
"Where is your wife and children?" asked Susan.
Abha reluctantly went to the kitchen and unable to stop her without reason, found Susan trotting close behind.
"I always ask her to stop working, but she never listens," said Abha defensively.
Susan walked past Abha and turned round to him saying gaily, "that's ok, I'll chat with your wife in here. I'm sure John has more questions for you."

"Her English is no good, I can translate."
That's ok, sir, we'll manage. And I have this young lady here," said Susan smiling down at me, "she will surely help us understand each other."
"She's just a child, she can't understand anything!"
"Yes, she is just a child, and a very clever child helping mummy with the housework already!"
Abha shrugged crossly, knowing that the scene was not looking good and it was better that he backed down now.

Susan looked at the tiny waif carrying a baby that seemed almost as long as her torso. Kaali remained downcast not wanting her husband seen in a bad light.
"Hello Karishma," said Susan sweetly to me.
I liked her immediately and smiled "Hello".
"I hear you are a clever young lady at school. Your mummy and daddy must be very proud of you."
An astute six-year-old does not start to blurt out how life really was because of the consequences, especially to her mother.
"Yes", I replied, "mummy and I go to the library sometimes."
This was not a lie; it had been true sometime back in the past. Susan smiled back then looked at Kaali and my little brother.
"Does he sleep at night?"
"Not always" replied Kaali.

"He seems to have a bad cold. Have you taken him to the doctor? In case he has an infection."

"No, it's just a little cold. I didn't think it was serious."

"Your husband was wrong. You speak English very well."

Kaali looked down, a glimmer of a smile flashed across her face.

"Did you not get the letters for the immunisations for your baby?"

Kaali shook her head, she was sure that Abha would not have prevented something as important as the vaccinations for the baby.

"Look I'll show you a copy."

Kaali looked at the letter from the clinic and immediately pointed out the error, "We live at number 14 not 17."

Susan looked in disdain, "oh my goodness, no wonder! I'm so sorry, it's completely our fault."

Kaali was relieved, hoping that Susan would now leave. But she chose to linger and probe further, "Are you eating enough and looking after yourself? It's always very difficult after a new baby."

Kaali nodded, "I'm fine. Just didn't sleep enough with the baby."

"Do you have family or friends close by who can help?"

Kaali was getting frustrated and never knowing how

to respond to interrogation. She closed her eyes and sighed. "I'm fine, thank you." She hugged Amit closer to her body and drew me close to her side. It was a signal to Susan not to come any closer with words or actions.

"Ok then, I'll speak to your husband to sort out a date for the clinic."

Back in the living room, John and Abha were chuckling and having a little banter about housework much to Susan's irritation.

"The letters have been sent to wrong address! Are you or your wife able to bring the baby to the clinic on Wednesday afternoon at 3 o'clock?"

"Yes of course! I can ask to leave work early."

Susan handed him a copy of the letters with the corrected address, apologised for the error, glared at John saying, "We should go now, we've wasted enough of Mr and Mrs Chetti's time."

She marched towards the door, John cross with her rather brusque manner, followed shaking Abha's hand. "It's been a pleasure meeting you, sir. Goodnight!"

The reason for the visit was not merely the absence at clinic appointments. Social Services had received an anonymous call stating that Mrs Chetti and her daughter were being abused by the husband.

"How dare you! The man is a potential wife beater

and you just sit and make fun of women and housework! You are despicable!"

"Calm down, Susan. I was merely putting him at ease and probing without making it obvious. You don't think if I interrogate him, he's just going to put his hands up and say, oh yes I beat up my wife and kids!"

"Well your methodology is utter rubbish! I've a good mind to report you."

"For goodness sake, stop being dramatic! Well, how was Mrs Chetti? Did she have bruises, was there anything suspicious?"

Susan sighed, "Oh God, she was so tiny. She looked malnourished and exhausted. Very subservient, there's no way she would admit to any wrong doings by her husband."

"You can't jump to conclusions. Lots of Asians are quite tiny and it's their culture where the male is accepted as the dominant force in the household. You know the old fashioned English way."

"It was more than that. I could feel there was something not quite right. She definitely seemed oppressed."

"Look you can't expect a different culture to just change overnight and behave in a way that's totally alien to them. Mr Chetti seemed on the surface to be a reasonable, likeable guy. I think probably he's just over protective with his family because it's a completely new life for them."

Susan shook her head.

"I don't want the file closed. I want to keep it open for a couple of more reviews."

"I don't think it's necessary and I don't agree. There are women and children in A & E every day with bruises and broken bones. This family does not fall into that category."

"Please let's keep it open for one more review at least. In say three months when we know that the family are attending clinics and the baby is in good health. I'm sure the anonymous call was for a reason"

"If that's what you want, fine. But I won't be coming and wasting my time."

So they agreed to disagree with Susan still having a vivid picture of the pitiful Kali in her mind.

CHAPTER 20

A few days later a letter arrived from India addressed to Kaali. It was from her youngest sister, Indira and read as follows:

My dearest sister
We all miss you very much and feel very sad since you had to leave us. Word came to us that you had left India and we had to beg your mother-in-law for your address.
Father is very ill and can no longer do any work and mother's eyesight is so bad she can hardly do anything at all. Pratibha has married to Shivan in the village and everything we had has been given to him as dowry. Her mother-in-law does not allow her to come and visit us.
Pragna cannot get married as she has to stay at home to look after father and mother but now she

seems to have some sort of sickness also. I am the only one who goes to work in our school as a teacher. I have a lot of respect here but the salary is not enough to look after everyone.

I have had some marriage proposals but father cannot afford the dowry. The boys here demand more and more these days.

We feel very happy that you are happily married and now living in England. Your mother-in-law cried when she talked about her new grandson.

Maybe you can help me to come to England so I can earn more money to help our parents. Also if you can send a postal order now and again to pay for the doctors' bills it would be very good. It is our duty to always look after our parents.

I hear that your husband sends money regularly to his mother. She is very lucky to have such a good son who does not forget her and still takes care of her. They have a nice big house; you have been very lucky but please don't forget your poor, sick family who always think of you.

Yours ever loving sister
Indira

Kaali was moved by the letter and tears streamed down as she remembered her sisters. It was true what Indira had written that she had a duty to her parents. However much they had scolded her, it was their right to reprimand her and they were still her parents. But her current precarious situation left her helpless and she dare not ask Abha for money to send to her parents. She knew he would refuse anyway.

Abha was still at work and Karishma at school. She lay on her bed snuggled up with the sleeping Amit her mind wracking for a solution for the impossible problem until finally sleep overpowered her exhausted mind.

A loud knocking on the door woke Kaali up with a start. She had fallen into a deep, much needed sleep and time had cast its spell. She carried the still sleeping Amit and peeped through a crack at the door. It was Joan with Carol and Karishma. Kaali shocked that she had overslept and failed to collect her daughter, patted her hand on her heart to express her profuse thanks.

"Are you alright, my dear? I thought something might have happened when you didn't turn up at the school gates."

"Thank you. Thank you so much. I didn't realise the time. So stupid!"

"You must be tired; it's always tiring with a new baby. Let me have a look at him."

Kaali, gently pulled the Amit away from her close embrace and let down the shawl to show the sleeping baby. He didn't stir and laid like a rag doll in his mother's arms.

Joan stroked his cheek, "Ooh, he's very cold."

It was a warm day and not even a cool breeze fluttered past.

Kaali gazed at her motionless child.

Joan's heart was beating, her inner voice told her that all was not right.

"Let's go in dear and put him down so that he's comfortable. Girls, you stay out here and play. Don't go to the edge of the pavement."

Kaali lay Amit down in the middle of the bed also feeling a little anxious that he had not woken up crying as he would normally. Joan held Kaali by the shoulders and looked at her square in the face.

"I don't think he's well, Kaali. I think we should call an ambulance."

Kaali was confused as to why Joan thought that her son was unwell.

Joan made the girls sit on the wall outside by the railings and ran to the phone box telling Kaali not to shut the door. She then phoned her husband to collect the girls as she dared not send Kaali alone in the ambulance. Kaali sleepwalked around the bed, finally resting on the edge looking down at Amit. He looked peaceful and beautiful. She looked at him as if it was the first time she had ever seen him in four months. He'd always been crying, his nose running, never sleeping for more than an hour at a time. They had gone to the clinic for the vaccination yesterday, but because of his cold they did not give it and had made a second appointment. Now his face was round and glowing with good health, she had never seen him looking so bonny. He did feel cold and his skin smooth like marble.

Within minutes Joan returned, trembling at the turn of events. The ambulance arrived soon after. She whispered to them and they gently took the baby and checked its breathing. They looked at Joan and shook their head.
"Dear God, why has this happened?" cried Joan. Kaali sat looking at Amit not understanding how sleep and death had become intertwined. Had she unknowingly killed him? How had she slept while her child had lain dying? Why was she still alive? They baby was carefully wrapped up with only a tiny part of his nose peeping through. Carol led Kaali towards the waiting ambulance and the sombre group made their way to the hospital.
Kaali thought of Abha and how he loved to play with Amit every morning and evening, even for the short while, it gave her joy to see that she had made him happy. She thought of Karishma, who was born from sin, distant in her approach to Abha and cautious in her communications with him. The thought that Amit may also have been conceived by brutal force was locked away in her mind, it was nobody's business but the curse that she had to live with.

Cases of infantile death syndrome were handled very delicately by the hospital as the police had to be involved. Kaali looked very unlike a child murderer but they had to keep her in hospital for questioning and follow the guidelines. They were kindly and sensitive in their efforts to glean the facts and doctors were called as they were concerned with her state of health and mind.

Abha was traced and brought in. Kaali watched him as he rolled on a hospital bed howling with grief. He had seen and held the tiny body, disbelief that his son, his pride and joy could just die with no warning. He had seen Kaali and if eyes had blades she would have been slaughtered there and then. He was furious and disgusted to see Joan in the background, she was always at a family scene before him. The doctors prescribed a mild sleeping tablet for Abha and he was taken home by a police officer. The constable said he would pay him a visit the next day for a chat and check that he was alright. Joan also left after hugging Kaali tearfully and promised to return the next morning with toiletries and anything else she may need. Kaali was still in shock and showed no emotion and had reverted to her silent existence deep in fear of her own cursed existence.

CHAPTER 21

Kaali was propped up in a hospital bed with a drip needled into her threadlike vein. Tests showed that she was malnourished and anaemic. They were astonished to understand how she had even carried herself on a daily basis. She had remained unresponsive to the death of her baby and had been shunned by her husband. Immediate emotions were always difficult to analyse especially without knowing the history behind the family. It was a truly tragic incident where the initial reaction was always to blame, blame each other, blame themselves and the cycle of mourning had to be experienced and never be forgotten. The wounds and scars would stay forever embedded in their hearts and lives.

The two police officers stood beside her bed and once again questioned her gently on her daily routine. Kaali responded calmly and coherently. It was not a difficult routine and every day was practically the same. There was no elaboration of the pressure or the exhaustion. She made life appear like a well-oiled machine.

"I killed my baby" she finally admitted in a flat monotone.

"How did you kill your baby?" asked the young police constable feeling very sorry for her.

"I went to sleep and he died. I didn't hear him cry. I didn't save him."

"You didn't kill him. The doctors are going to perform an autopsy to find the cause of death. Sometimes babies die for no known reason. We'll let you rest and come back tomorrow."

Kaali lay in the whiteness of the hospital room looking up at the ceiling. She thought of Abha alone in the flat, seeing him grieving for his dead son. She thought of Karishma, her little soldier who dealt with life's traumas just as she did. She thought of her little bundle, Amit and his short life. She barely knew him, he had just been this incessantly crying doll which she had carried around. All the countless sins she had committed in her life time, it was relentless. But this had to be the largest sin of all where she slept while her child lay dying. She wondered why she had not died too. She had escaped death throughout her lifetime several times and with each survival the feelings of self-disgust increased.

Back in the flat, Abha lay on his bed broken hearted at the thought of his Amit now gone. What riled Abha more than anything was the calm subdued manner of Kaali. She was able to interact and have conversations with others but not him. He had tried on the ship but to no avail, she had always remained frustratingly silent and aloof. He had never been able to reduce her to tears. The more he lashed out, the stronger she seemed. Her endurance seemed limitless. He saw it as arrogance that she did not acknowledge his strength. She would simply bow down or kneel, almost challenging him to strike and strike again. If she had cried or begged him for mercy, he would have had pity on her and rewarded her for her humility.

He lay groaning unable to contain his emotions, clenched his hands and as they pounded on the pillow, he felt the hardness of an object underneath. He was lying on the very same pillow on which his son had died. The object was Kaali's little goddess, Abha flung it against the wall uncertain of the significance of this ugly statue. Also under the pillow he found the letter sent by Indira.
His fury quadrupled when he read the contents not even checking the date. Had she been secretly

sending money without his consent to the very same family who had thrust this misfortune upon him, the family who had denounced her and threatened to kill her. He wanted to lay his bare hands round Kaali's neck there and then and throttle the life out of her.

Finally, each in their own bed fell into a haunting asleep where one wished to die and one wished to kill.

CHAPTER 22

I was in a magical world, far removed from the drama of death and the dark days and nights.
I shared Carol's precious bedroom of pink bejewelled wind chimes and a basket of ribbons and hair clips. We played imaginative games with her dolls and teddies where everyone lived happily ever after. The worst tragedy that ever happened was a teddy would have a bad arm and needed bandaging. Carol taught me what childhood was all about and I taught Carol the wonders of books and knowledge. We would lay on the floor immersed in Hans Christian Anderson fairy tales or the adventures of the Famous Five. We would finger through catalogues calculating our balance after our very extravagant purchases from our million-pound bank balance.

I barely thought of my family.
Abha was just an existence to be wary of and obeyed. The closer knit family days aboard the Streathden were like a surreal dream. Amit was sweet but took up nearly all of my mother's time, I never resented him but felt sad for the loss of our precious moments.

I totally and unconditionally loved and respected Kaali and would have done so even if she had not been my mother. However, I did not understand her. I did not see her as weak but I did not understand her acceptance and tolerance of the treatment she received at the hands of Abha. I knew that she loved me but sometimes wondered if she would have sacrificed me if that was what Abha wished. I could not think of any single moment where she had defied Abha such was her commitment and devotion to him.

I spent five glorious days and nights with Carol. Joan would put us in the bath together every evening, a large tin bath placed in the middle of the kitchen floor. Nothing seemed as arduous or as punishing as at home. Being tucked into bed after a hot chocolate, a story and songs and finally a cuddle was like being in heaven. I will always remember Joan for the love and warmth she showered on me. The kind words to reassure me when she sensed I

was feeling unsure or insecure. She would laugh as she struggled to control my thick black mane and threatened to cut it off and make herself a wig with it. Laughter was the most natural action and reaction to almost everything in the Levene household.
On the sixth day, Wednesday, Joan told me that Kaali was much better and would be coming back home from the hospital. She had not been able to contact Abha and messages posted into his letter box had been unanswered. The hospital also told her that he had not returned to the hospital to visit Kaali, but had been guided through the process of cremation which he had requested for his son. The autopsy did not show any definitive reason for the cause of death except that the baby had just stopped breathing, apparently an occasional inexplicable occurrence.

Kaali's weak body had also been resurrected from death's door and she looked healthier and stronger than ever before in her lifetime. So Joan took it upon herself to collect Kaali and booked a taxi to bring her back home safe. She kept me at home with Carol and her father until she could ensure that all was well in our flat.

However, once reaching our flat, Kaali hugged Joan with small sobs and tremors unable to fathom the depth of kindness shown from someone who had once been a stranger. She shook her head begging Joan not to come in and that she had to go in alone and face whatever lay before her. These words were not spoken just understood. Joan was not happy, having taken a dislike to the devious Abha, but understanding the trauma of losing their baby was something that they had to deal with.

"I'll bring Kari back after tea about six tonight. Then you can get her straight to bed and not worry about her. I'll collect her tomorrow morning at eight and take her to school. You should take the rest of the week a little easier."

Kali hugged her again and let her go with a heavy heart. She shut the door and ventured slowly inside not knowing what was now expected of her by Abha or the gods.

Abha sat in his usual armchair watching television and drinking beer. Her entrance had no impact on his focus. She fell to her knees and lay her forehead on the floor, cautiously edging towards him. He flicked her aside with a sharp kick and carried on watching TV. Kaali rose dejected and dragged herself to the kitchen where she found the room in turmoil with dirty plates and greasy containers from takeaways. It was joy to see this chaos and have a sense of purpose. As if a switch had been turned on, she busied herself scrubbing and cleaning. She checked the provisions and cooked a meal for Abha. Her energy, replenished by the hospital's good care, knew no limits. She took his meal to him on a tray and lay it before him. She stripped both the bedrooms, not even glancing at the baby shawls or clothes, just throwing them into a corner, cleaned, dusted and laid clean sheets. She found her little goddess still intact but with a crack along the side of the face and hid it in the small room under the bed. She found her letter from Indira torn into pieces and put these together with her statue to be mended later.

She saw that Abha had eaten his meal and left the tray on the floor, she was about to pick it up when the doorbell rang. She automatically ran to the door, knowing it would be Joan bringing me back to my rightful place. Abha looked up startled at the speed that she went to the door and even more startled that she should dare to presume that she should be allowed to open the door in the first place. But he said nothing, everything was being mentally documented.

I was taken straight to the bedroom hugged and left. Kaali went back to clear the tray and when she could find nothing else to occupy her, she too joined me and we both snuggled back in bed with our books like the old days.

CHAPTER 23

Life was once again like clockwork, cooking, cleaning, sewing and school runs. Kaali saw to Abha's needs, she wasted nothing and the only attention she awarded me was our walks to and from school and at bedtime when she dared to lay down her head to rest. She lingered over combing my hair in the morning, but out of sight of Abha's watchful eyes. Joan had given me some ribbons which always stayed in my pocket lest they get hidden or thrown away for any trivial reason.

Abha remained silent. There were no more torrents of verbal abuse. No more drunken dribble. No insults about the cooking, cleaning or the laundry. It was as if he two ghosts lived alone side by side, aware of each other's existence but feared to tread in each other's path.

Kaali and I never touched the television any more. We never ate or drank in front of Abha.
My plate was served on the kitchen floor on a mat where I ate. I never saw Kaali eat or drink or a single word pass her lips in Abha's presence. The doomed household's mood weighed down on me and I began to dread weekends and school holidays where there was nowhere to escape. The complexity of my mother's mind and the cruelty of my father's was beyond reasoning for a six-year-old. I would draw stick pictures of Abha and then tear them into little pieces and stamp on them. I wished him dead, the blight that he was on our lives. The padlock to my mind had been unlocked by the exposure to a happy family life and I now knew that our current existence was ugly and I detested every moment in that basement tomb.

Another silent Friday evening ensued where I was in bed reading and Kaali as always in the kitchen scrubbing something or other or herself. She would only use cold water. Boiled water was only reserved for me or Abha. If there had ever been a saint anointed for self- persecution or base humility it would have been Kaali.

The dreaded doorbell rang. Nobody moved. Kaali stood in a corner in the kitchen waiting and listening. Abha did not move and carried on watching TV as if nothing was amiss.

The bell rang again.

Abha spoke flatly, no emotion, "Open the door". Kaali obeyed, pulling her veil over her head as she passed through the living room into the corridor.

"Hello" said Susan Johnstone smiling and beside her was John Barrett.

"We were really sorry to hear the sad news and just came to offer some support." said John.

"It's ok" said Kaali, "we're managing", not opening the door any more than a crack.

"Can we please come in?"

"My husband is tired. We are alright, thank you."

Disappointed, Susan and John walked away, but glad that it was Kaali who had opened the door. She looked reasonably well and in fact better than the last time that they had seen her. Susan agreed with John that there was no apparent risk and the file should be closed.

Abha heard every word and sat uncommenting even when Kaali passed through back to the kitchen. She brought him a mug of steaming hot spiced tea to comfort and warm him then sat on the kitchen floor rocking herself until she heard him go to bed. Only then did she creep into our bed and allow herself to rest.

Friday evening came and Kaali had cooked a nutritious and spicy chicken and vegetable soup which she had made with giblets that Abha had brought in the previous day. It was simmering over the paraffin heater, the tempting aroma even banishing the paraffin fumes. Kaali served me a bowl with bread and butter and I sat on the kitchen floor munching away, dunking my bread. The taste and smell of home cooking was the only missing pleasure at Carol's house. Joan made some substantial meals but I was practically getting withdrawal systems form having no spice in my diet. The nearest they got to anything spicy was a coronation chicken sandwich which I found very difficult to muster, but I was so well trained in behaviour that they would never have guessed the difficulty I had in swallowing this.

I wished Kaali and I could have watched some television together or snuggled in bed and read. But I knew she would not leave the kitchen until Abha came home. So once again I left the silent kitchen and got into bed with a copy of Grimm's Fairy tales where every fairy had my elfin face and in every tale I was the heroine. I waved my arm about with my imaginary wand and transformed the bedroom into a glass palace. I would take out Kaali's little statue and this would be the evil queen who would be intent on casting spells to ensure that the prince did not live. But then I with my magic wand would bring the witch down to her knees and banish her from the castle forever. The little prince and I would then dance and live together happy ever after.

Every chapter in one's life needs a reason for existence just as every chapter in a book needs a reason to be written. Events are not purely by chance. There was an inevitability in Kaali's life that every event lead to humiliation and blight. Every glimmer of hope appeared as a cunning ploy to trick Kaali into another dark abyss. Then there are the blessed ones whose paths calamity dare not cross and there is no wretchedness in the air they breathe.

Kaali's reason for existence was to serve others and punish herself. She was born a sinner and every act was more evidence of her condemned life. I felt, even in my young bones, that my path would not be determined by others. The early chapters of my life were an education of what was possible. I had seen children in the playground being carried on their shoulders by their fathers. I envied the reckless conversations by the parents in the playground and children running around with total abandonment. Finally, my book world and my dream world collided and I fell into a deep slumber, having given up on Kaali coming to hold me.

Kaali remained in the kitchen to well after midnight until it seemed apparent that Abha wasn't coming home. She was unsure what to do. In the old days she would have just cried herself to sleep on the kitchen floor as she remembered back in Devi's kitchen. She was no longer able to cry, even when she wanted the release of the compacted tears in her heart. She did the practical things of putting away the food in the fridge. Turning the paraffin heater off. It wasn't really cold but Kaali turned on the heater just before she thought Abha was due back to take out the chill from the room or if she was cooking the never ending cheap broths.

She stepped out of the front door, peering into the darkness to see if there was any sign of Abha. After about ten minutes of turning her head in every direction, she finally resorted to accepting that he may have stayed overnight with friends from work and he would surely be back in the morning. She came to bed with a heavy heart, worried about his safety, praying that he had not been drinking too much and had had an accident. She needed sleep and had not eaten anything. She only ate after Abha had eaten. If Abha had searched the whole world over, he would never have found another woman who would have been as caring and devoted as

Kaali and would have sacrificed anything for his happiness.

She resolved to be patient and not panic until he turned up and also see if Joan was able to look after me while she roamed the roads she knew he frequented whether it was to go to work or to do the shopping.

Abha was right, she no longer had any fear as such. She did not have the fear of a frightened animal but she did fear losing Abha and failing as a wife.

CHAPTER 24

Saturday morning and still no sign of Abha. My stoic attitude was unencumbered by any anxieties of his presence or absence. I feasted on the leftovers for breakfast sitting on the kitchen floor across from Kaali. Each mouthful she placed between her lips was as if she was feeding herself with pebbles from a muddy river. It was only the mug of sweet tea which she cupped between her aged hands that was sipped like a nectar from paradise. She languished over clearing up in her hapless manner and forgot my existence, absorbed in the foul whisperings in her ears. I slipped away to the comfort of my bed reading my books and writing my own magical story in my romantic heart.

By midday, I was getting restless, missing school, missing company. Kaali was sitting on the kitchen floor, gently rocking with eyes closed. I touched her cheek and startled her and saw the utter desolation in her eyes. I sat on her lap and wrapped my skinny arms around her, burying my face in her neck. The remembrance of my existence and the guilt of ignoring me brought a choking gasp from her throat as she too wrapped her arms around me and held me tight.

"Can I read to you, please?" I whispered.

Kaali cocked her head puzzled, but allowed me to lead her by the hand back to the bedroom. She slid under the blanket but I sat in front of her as the bed was my stage.

I read the story of Rapunzel with my arms waving about profusely and swishing my plaits, expressions to capture the characters in my reading. To my amazement, Kaali burst out laughing. It was the first time I had ever heard her laugh out aloud and I carried on inspired to draw more mirth from my beloved mother. My acting became more exaggerated until at the end I collapsed on her shoulders laughing in sheer childish glee.

Feeling emboldened I asked, "Can we go to the park and the library?"

I had missed our walks through the park and occasionally being treated to an ice cream. I missed sitting together in our book world, where I would

nudge Kaali to show an illustration or she would point out a word to ask me the meaning.
She looked at me dolefully but agreed.

Out in the fresh air, the sun glinting through the houses and trees, the world was far removed from our basement flat or even my grandmother's kitchen. We walked with tiny hand in tiny hand and sat on a park bench watching people and imagining the homes that they would return to. The care and petting that dogs received intrigued us. They would trot cutely on their leads following their master or mistress without ever being their slave. The owners would hug, kiss and reprimand them as if they were boisterous little toddlers. To my delight we saw Joan and Carol walking towards us. Carol ran the last few paces,
"Come on Kari let's go on the swings."
I looked at Kaali who smiled and nodded and we ran off with Joan calling after us to take care.
"How are you my dear? I do worry about you and think of you all the time."
"I'm managing okay, Joan. But I'm worried. My husband didn't come home last night."

Kaali never complained or confided in anything personal and Joan respected that although she could not understand it. Joan liked the sound of Kaali's voice. Her Indian accent, with little intonation gave her tones a quiet elegance, but with a childlike honesty.

"Maybe he just needs to be alone for a while. He could just be staying with a work friend or something."

"Should I not be looking for him or going to the police?"

"I think wait until the weekend's over. Maybe you should take this time to spend with Kari. You both need some quality time together."

Kaali sighed, she knew that she neglected me and it had always been that way. She didn't know how that had become her pattern of behaviour. She tried to think back to her own childhood and remembered nothing. She could not remember her childhood. She wondered if she had ever had a childhood and now she was depriving her daughter of the love and care she deserved.

"Ok. I'll wait and see until Monday."

Carol and I came running back as the tinkle of the ice cream van was heading towards the park.

"Come on girls, what a pair! You both have ears as big as an elephant!"

She wandered off to join the ever increasing clamour of children around the van while Kaali sat watching, not quite understanding how people were so carefree and happy. How easily they chattered and laughed. They had no fear of going home. They had no fear of being happy or being punished for their happiness.

Joan's chatter was also infectious. Kaali found herself being lured from her self-made tomb to tug at my plaits or pinch my cheek until we all finally parted in good humour.
We entered our basement cautiously in case my devil father had returned. He was not there. Kaali floated through to the kitchen nodding me to follow her. Swiftly, she peeled potatoes, chopped onions and got on doing what she loved best. She made a dough from the chapatti flour and gave me dough balls to shape as I please. I shaped these into the sun, the moon, a witch's hat and a funny face. This was the childhood I wanted and savoured every moment with adult awareness, suspecting that when Abha came back, it would never happen again.

We ate our early evening meal and retired to the bedroom, still not daring to use the living room or switch on the television. Kaali took out her little statue and gave it a good polish and was trying to put together the fragmented letter. I took out one of my ribbons, a gay red one and tied it round the statue's waist with a big bow at the back. Again Kali laughed, I saw how beautiful and transformed her face was every time she smiled or laughed. Her slightly upward tilting eyes, veiled by her long lashes, looked almost alluring and magnetic when they were not dark circles of despair and hopelessness.

I helped her put the letter back together using a flour paste as glue and together we wrote a reply.

My dearest sister Indira
My heart was full of joy when I received your letter. I thought the family all hated me and had forgotten me. May God bless you for looking after our parents. It must be very hard for you. I want to help you and father and mother and I will find a way. What is wrong with Pragna? Life is difficult at the moment but I will find a way to send some money to help with the medical bills.
Getting married in the village is always very hard. I am indeed blessed that my husband took pity on me and do my best to serve him as a good wife.
We have been through a difficult time at the moment, but Abha has kindly got me a sewing machine so that I can work from home. I will save some money and send to you as soon as I can.
Yours ever loving sister
Kaali

There was no further elaboration needed or the mention of my existence. The letter was to ask for money but to Kaali this was a letter that proved she was missed and needed.

She tucked me into bed with a book and sat at the sewing machine in the living room, putting together sleeves or collars or whatever was in the next batch. Her mind counted and calculated on how she could syphon some of the earnings into a separate pot.

The man came every Sunday evening, with a new batch, collected and counted the old and paid the wage. She felt sure that Abha would return in time for the money which was put directly into his hand. She pondered on how she could arrange a second visit during the weekday or would she dare ask for her dinner lady job back.

She churned away the pieces, her sewing machine humming away, counting the pieces and calculating the income. In her ordinarily open and honest life, she was not wily enough to be deceitful and cunning. But she sewed most of the evening and most of Sunday, catching up with the days she had lost direction determined to make her parents happy.

Mr Khan arrived Sunday evening at 7pm as normal. Abha was still not home. Kali without a fuss, told him the number of pieces completed and the amount that was owed.

"Where is your husband?" Mr Khan leered.
"He will be home soon, just gone to the shops."
Mr Khan disappointed, swapped the batches and paid the money. Kaali thought it not wise for him to return when she was alone so said nothing further.

I had a glorious weekend, fearless in wandering around our flat, going through old newspapers and cutting out paper dolls, singing hymns and songs I had learnt at school and even being allowed to comb and plait my mother's hair.

I was in bed by 7.30 on Sunday evening hoping that Monday would arrive early so I could get back to school. I wanted to play hopscotch in the playground and put my hand up in class, proudly being able to put it up the fastest for the times table quiz.

Monday did arrive and Kaali took me to school, both of us mentally refreshed and lighter in step. Whereas I would normally run off to find Carol, Kaali held me back and stooped down and held me close.
"Study well, my little rani"
I smiled giving her a quick hug back and ran off without a backward look.
She waved and went back home.

CHAPTER 25

Back in the flat, Kaali rushed around repeatedly cleaning the immaculate flat. Abha's bed was smoothed down with clean sheets and blankets. The living room dusted and the carpet scrubbed with a dustpan and brush, the food preparation complete so that the cooking could be done at a moment's notice.

She sat down to start sewing, deftly shaping and trimming each piece, neat piles on either side of her as she shifted the load and counted the earnings. Her takings from yesterday lay under her pillow, undecided on how she was going to hold some back without Abha noticing.

Her heart missed a beat when she heard the key in the lock. She ran to the kitchen and stood in the corner, relieved that he had returned but gripped in fear. She heard him sink into his armchair and rapidly put the kettle on to boil. She wondered why he was not at work and whether he had eaten breakfast or lunch. She brought him a cup of tea which he took with no thanks.

He had seen that Kaali had been busy sewing.
"Where's the money?"
Kaali quickly went to get the small roll of banknotes and on impulse, put one back under her pillow. She started to edge back to the kitchen when he shouted, "Stop! Sit down!"
She sat on the floor while he counted the notes and the few loose coins which she had produced. He looked puzzled and recounted,
"Why that dirty Khan has given me short!"

He looked at Kaali remembering the letter from her sister. She sat trembling, too frightened to confess. He got up and looked at her closely in the face.
"Are you trying to swindle me? You filthy wretch you're stealing from me to send to your nasty family!"
Kaali shook her head desperately trying to beg forgiveness from her dying throat.
"You killed my son! You steal from me! You ruin my life and bring misery to it every single day!"

Abha was now in full swing and gave vent to an incoherent stream of abuse, slapping her head with each accusation as if possessed by demons. Kaali still sat, swaying with each blow, no longer trembling, clamouring for the blows to ease her pain and guilt. He saw the glint of the scissors by the sewing machine and grabbed them raising the blades above her with both his hands. Kaali gasped with longing and ripped bare her breast and opened her arms to welcome death.

Even whilst immersed in his hatred, growing was a jealousy of her hidden strength, her actions froze him. She knelt before him, eyes wide open, not like a quivering mouse but a strong lioness, embracing the anticipation of the cold, shining blades. The fear now was all his and he was terrified by her strength and flung the scissors, convulsing in his own spit. He lifted her up, grabbing her face with his single hand, his grip so tight that he could almost feel his fingers touch each other through her cheeks. He brought his face close up to hers hissing out "Evil bitch!"

His eyes were bloodshot with unleashed fury as he flung her against the wall, lifting her with his single hand into the air. He kicked her one final time and charged out of the room, slamming the door to escape from demons that chased him.

Kaali lay in a heap, stunned, absorbing the pain. She lay there with cracked ribs waiting for more. She heard him snap shut his suitcase and finally slam the front door and leave.

She lay there for some hours, breathing shallow, in and out of a comatose state. She dragged herself, an inch at a time to give herself some reprieve from the stabbing pains in her chest. It was her hardy endurance that finally lifted her on to the bed where she lay at death's door.

She did not want to live, not even for me, her own daughter, Karishma. In her depraved soul she was an unworthy mother and her existence had been pointless and a punishment for all around her. It had been hell on earth and she deserved hell in the hereafter, such was her inherent belief.

She felt for her little goddess, now decked in a red ribbon, lifted her head and brushed it with her lips. Her dark lashes cast shadows across her high cheekbones and flickered no longer. She knew that this would be her last breath and prayed to God for forgiveness for all her sins. She thought of the river and the flowing waters where she had wanted to submerge herself and give up on life. It seemed like surreal dream and now she was at death's door and her wish had finally been granted.

END OF PART ONE

KARI

PART TWO

Revenge is mine,

Blood is sweet.

I won't rest, until you die.

CHAPTER 1

There were five children around the table eating shepherd's pie with boiled cabbage and gravy. We varied in sizes and ages of between six and fourteen, I being the youngest. The eldest, Tom, swore and banged his cutlery on the table to assert his authority. I had very quickly learnt not to look at him as he invited reasons to start a fight. He thrived on conflict and drama. He had an open, aggressive attitude with his underlying agenda too complex for the staff to analyse or cope with. His accomplice, Ben, needed Tom for his bodyguard and status. He was not physically strong like Ben but had a mean streak. He knew how to manipulate Tom and create mayhem for his own titillation. They formed a strong bond, depending on each other's strengths, Ben the brains and Tom the muscle, neither of them willing to show any signs of vulnerability or weakness. Mercy had no fear and her moods were as volatile as Tom's. She was one of the few who showed no fear to the menacing pair and they in turn chose to eliminate her from their taunting. I sat between Mercy and Julie, the latter being disinterested in life itself, her apparent apathy being her armour.

We should have been a group of children, chattering nonsense that youngsters do, being cared for and protected by the teachers. But this was no ordinary school. This was a home full of unwanted children, who carried around the baggage and the thwarted dreams of their parents. Did anyone ever ask me what I wanted or how I truly felt? Of course not, they were too frightened or uninterested to hear the truth. I was in the system, spoken to kindly, constantly reassure that I would be taken good care of. Their intentions were well meant but their words and actions maintained a distance for their own protection. My head was patted and occasionally I was given a hug. But I was just really another case, held at arm's length, passing through with no real connection.

Despite Joan's pleas to be able to foster me and give me a home, the decision was that she would not be able to support me with my cultural or religious needs. In fact, they moved me as far away as possible to Derby as no suitable places were available in the London children's homes. The initial spate of childish letters from Carol were killed off by me as I had nothing to write as the truth was too ugly. I was not afraid of violence as I had witnessed enough from Abha, although his physical threats had never been directed at me. The death of my mother was still a deep bleeding wound that had not been stemmed. I refused to open up to questioning by therapists and psychologists. My inability to understand and express my innermost thoughts was interpreted as trauma that would heal with time and counselling was withdrawn as being ineffective. Abha, my father had deserted me and disappeared. It seemed dubious that he was even still in the country.

The conclusion I reached at the age of six was that the only person I could count on was myself. There were two parts to my personality that developed as two separate individuals. The outer self for the world was the obedient, intelligent little girl who was little trouble and had an amenable character. The inner self that I cultivated was shrewd and calculating and I did not suffer fools or allow herself to be affected by the domination or bullying. I absorbed and analysed the characters that ran around me like little hamsters on a treadmill. They were all eager to find the right partner or 'friend' or simply remain as invisible as possible. Interestingly,

I found the staff also followed the same pattern for survival, even with having the upper hand, they would still wrongfully collude with those they had the most affinity with.

The groups and gangs that formed in the home were crucial to our survival. Everyone had to belong but life would still be difficult for the weakest. It was not just the wanton children that created fear but also some of the depraved staff who guarded their property, which was mainly a selection of children, with an iron fist.

I sensed that Ben had already taken a dislike to me spitting out cutting remarks any time he passed by. "Fucking Paki!" he'd sneer.
Or he would get Tom to rush past me and knock me down which would have everyone laughing hysterically. No one would dare to offer me a hand in case they would be at the receiving end of the next blow. The staff would look the other way or 'tut tut' in a meaningless gesture.

It was at mealtimes and weekends that the weakest had to be on guard, the onsite schooling was a welcome break although our academic ability was irrelevant. School holidays were an absolute nightmare, where there was more than one bleeding and bruised child each day. The excruciating pain I would suffer when the bullies stamped on my feet, my tiny bones were probably broken and healed more than once. I must have had the tough resistance of my mother for I did not cry and did not report any incident.

However, I was gradually building an invisible electrifying fence around me. There would be limits and there would be revenge. I kept a low profile but not like the servile presence of Kaali. I did not believe that I was a sinner like she or that my birth and existence was to be merely tolerated.

In some ways, I had pity for most of the children, even Tom and Ben, knowing that they either had no parents or had parents who had shunned, beaten or abused them. They had all built self-protecting mechanisms to cope with their sad, ugly lives. The children were comparatively easy; it was the adults that we all feared.

CHAPTER 2

Mr Baden was the most hated of all. He was a short round man who looked like a cuddly Santa Claus. His demeanour was the jolly absent-minded grandfather. The new children, as there was a constant conveyor belt where new entrants arrived or older ones transferred, were nearly always hoodwinked into complicity much to their shame and regret. Mr Baden would socialise with us about once a month during our evening meal, wandering from table to table. He would crack lame jokes and tease us, slapping our backs guffawing with laughter. He would offer particular attention to an individual of his choice and express concern either that they had not received a family visit or they had been injured in a childish brawl. He would stroke their hair with his short podgy fingers, consoling them and offering them comfort. Some of his older recruits would pander to his needs in exchange for cigarettes, drugs and alcohol. Those were their only expressions of pleasure and a sense that they had some power and control of their situation. Equally some of the staff would be smirking, aware of the selection process and finding the situation entertaining or even highlighting a child that they had a grievance with.

Some staff would look the other way or interact with him in a completely starchy, professional manner. The adults were accomplished in living a lie and found it acceptable to deny the truth.

I had had a particularly bad day. My small toe had been bleeding and was extremely sore. I had been limping for most of the day. Mrs Connor asked me if I had hurt myself knowing full well that I had been brutally stamped upon. I shrugged my shoulders and said it was nothing. As I limped past, Mr Baden stopped me and asked to have a look at my foot and insisted that Mrs Connor should follow in case any first aid needed to be administered. The swollen, bleeding toe was cleaned up and bandaged.

"You poor little thing, you should have said something." said Mr Baden in a concerned manner. "I know there are some little thugs in here, but you mustn't be frightened to report anything."

I didn't answer, just nodded my head.
He bent down and held my face in his hands, "Promise you'll come to me if ever you have a problem?"
Again I just nodded, eager to escape.
"Off you go, pet," he beamed, patting my bottom as I flew past.

The rest of the evening found me rather anxious but relieved that my toe had been dressed. I had heard whisperings of Mr Baden's attentions and felt repulsion by his sickly bedside manner and lay low for the rest of the evening.

It was a welcome command when the young ones were sent to bed at eight o'clock. Not all obeyed the lax rules that were in place but for some of us it gave a sense of security. Most of the children still subconsciously craved for discipline and boundaries. My reading habits had not left me and I was allowed to read for about half an hour before someone came in to switch off the lights.

A sombre gloom filled the room from the streetlight outside. All doors were kept slightly ajar and the noise from the older children diminished as they all slipped into their beds exhausted from another battling day.

In my nightly visions of a battered mother punched into my fragile sleep, a shadow loomed over me. Mr

Baden had slipped into my room, swaggering with his bullish frame, sniggering and lording over my puny, childish body.

"You're the lucky one today," he laughed softly, "what a pretty little thing you are!"

He put a finger to his lips to silence me, as if I didn't know enough about silence already. I stared back at him with vacant eyes, the hairs rising as my body chilled and sweated at the same time. I did not move a muscle but my heart was beating like the wings of a sparrow trapped in a rusted cage. He stooped over me and placed his index finger on my lips. I still dared not move and stared unblinking, feeling his warm sickly breath on my face. His other hand reached under the blanket and fumbled trying to loosen my pyjamas.

I was not my mother. My strength and resolve burst open with terror. I raised my leg and kicked him hard in his groin. He staggered back in shock and I screamed out, a loud piercing blood curdling scream as I pushed him away. He fell back against the wall, his arms knocking down a framed photo. It came crashing down, the plastic frame cracking. He stood back up regaining his balance but still wobbling in his oversized armour. My eyes were dark and threatening and Mr Baden, still in shock and confusion of losing power, had him wide eyed and grunting in anger. I was now unstoppable and leapt out of bed and lunged at him with all my bodily force. He fell back once more and only just managed to keep his balance against the wall.

Mrs Connor came running in and guessed what he had been up to. She had no wish to confront him or acknowledge that anything was amiss. Her inability to deal with abuse, especially with a senior management figure, was quite common among the staff.

"Kari! Kari! Calm down! It's okay, Mr Baden, Kari probably just had a bad dream. I'll see to her. I hope you're not hurt."

Mr Baden grunted and waddled out, hands in his pockets, seething with anger. She simply tucked me back into bed, "It's alright, dear. It's only a cheap picture, I'll see if I can find you a nicer one. Now say a little prayer, that'll help you sleep."

She picked up the cracked frame and left, detaching herself from what might have been and what she knew had happened many times before.

The next morning brought a silent respect from the other children, a hint of a smile or a nod of approval. News had travelled fast, even some of the most depraved staff eyed me suspiciously.

Ben silently passed something to me under the dining table wrapped in a newspaper, which I eased into my shoe to look at later. Tom walked behind me giving me a slap on the back and putting up his thumbs in approval. It felt good to have them on my side and to have shown my tough side which had so far never been revealed. Even I was astounded at my own courage and felt the power that was within me. In the toilets, I opened up the newspaper and found a short sharp flick-knife. I loved the blade and ran it close along my arm feeling the sting, but stopped short of drawing blood. I knew that in future I would relish using this on anyone who dared to invade my space or demean my presence. I would polish the blade carefully every night and keep it wrapped under my pillow and wear it inside my shoe or a belt during the day.

After that I kept a look out for objects that would serve as weapons from a nail file to a jagged stone and imagined how I could use them and what pain I could inflict. It became an obsessive and secretive hobby with an increased awareness of pain and death as I practised my dark art on nature's creatures.

Needless to say I was transferred to another home after a few weeks, after only having spent six months there, with a recommendation that I should be closely monitored and a mild sedative administered as I had recurring nightmares that disturbed the other children. My apparent aggressive behaviour was also highlighted as a result of my upbringing in an abusive home.

CHAPTER 3

The years linked into each other like shackles around my ankles, each year much the same, different personalities, different buildings but essentially the same nomadic existence learning the survival skills in a very depressive adult world. There were some longer periods in some of the homes, the longest being for almost two years. But there was still no stability and my reputation as a maladjusted and dangerous individual prevented any sort of meaningful friendships.

Control from the gate keepers came in many forms, malicious threats, physical beatings, emotional abuse and medication. There was no trust and any sensitivity was expressed with caution.

Medication was the easiest and most popular method of control if spirits rose too high and disturbances became threatening. Some of us got the art of how to hold a tablet at the back of the throat, only to thrust two fingers later and vomit it out. Mimicking those who had already been drugged was no difficult. However, if we were found out, they would then resort to the other forms of punishment. This could be a mere slap that smarted across the face or a member of staff would hold you down while others would throw in the tablet followed by a bucket of water down your throat or simply at your face. There was no escape for bad behaviour or reward for good behaviour. I was known for my loud piercing screams if anyone dared to cross me, but increasingly, I would stay silent and brandish a knife from my growing collection. I was quite the heroine and my small frame stood taller and stronger than any of my 'inmates'.

I stood out fiercely quiet and while others grew in height with maturing faces, I remained petite with childlike features.

I was not popular with the staff who thought I was arrogant and pompous. They looked at me disdainfully and were extremely irritated if they caught me reading. One staff member, Joe, who was possibly illiterate except for the basics, would snatch my book and slam it against my head. "Who do you think you are? Einstein!"

He would then fling the book into a corner and wander off laughing. His type did not worry me and I chose not to react to his feeble attempts to put me down. But I had a few faithful followers and my collection of blades and weapons grew as did my adeptness at wielding and puncturing my practice targets. I could behead a field mouse with one chop of a blade and found it fascinating when the body could still run off headless for a few seconds before it finally quivered and died. It was rumoured amongst the inmates that even as a young child I could deftly slice off a frog's leg before it leapt. Such was my notoriety. I was continually training myself, intent to desensitise my emotions to the pain of others with each stab or swipe of my blade. We were often left to wander the surrounding grounds where we would hound each other in our packs.

I was fourteen when I was eventually allocated to a foster family. I packed my possessions, the black statue still adorned with a red ribbon, the glued letter from my aunt Indira, my mother's and my passport which were of course now out of date and my secret stash of weapons poked into pockets and corners of my bag. The Asian clothes, which no longer interested me or fitted me, I promptly threw in the bin. My hair was cut short and in the main I wore jeans and t-shirts.

I liked wearing make-up and with the other girls, we all did our best to look older than our years in preparation for when we finally leave.

I was looking forward to the next morning to actually leaving the institutional lifestyle and curious as to how my new home would be.

My foster family were called Evie and Derek Foster. They were already fostering three other children and I would be their fourth. Evie and Derek were an energetic middle aged couple who had no children of their own. They showered attention upon us and gave us an organised structure to our daily lives.

We always ate breakfast and the evening meal together at the dining table. We were allocated chores to help around the house, with the exception of the youngest, Dennis, who was a two-year-old toddler.

Much to my delight, we were enrolled at the local school, the other two boys, James and Colin, aged eight and ten were not so enthusiastic. I loved helping with the domestics, playing with Dennis and sitting with James and Colin to help them with their homework.

Evie and Derek thought the world of me and although they had been given my background information, its inaccuracies which were thankfully irrelevant, they took me at face value. They initially guarded me when I was with the younger children as no doubt my reports would have included knifing incidents, but gradually they grew to trust me.

It was a cosy family life that we all settled into. We were taken to the park every Sunday after lunch, no matter what the weather was. We had regular visits from Social Services who still had the upper hand and made all decisions on my behalf.

On the surface, my life was now with foundation and purpose. I had already grown in stature and confidence but felt duty bound to my mother to try to make something of my life. I was polite and respectful to Evie and trusted her, but had little time for Derek, who just seemed a weak figure who shadowed the background. They had fostered many, many children throughout their lifetime so I knew that I was just a passing ghost. But I strived to give back for all the care and attention they afforded me. I confided certain elements of my past memories, such as memories of Carol and Joan. Evie promptly bought me a letter writing pad, envelope and stamps the next day. I wanted to get my passport renewed, but this was out of their hands and I would have to wait until I was eighteen or ask Social services to support.

I would have dark moods when I would relive the past memories of the pain inflicted on Kaali. I would get angry for having looked away or distanced myself from the beatings. I should have screamed then, or confided in Joan for help or any of the teachers. I could have stopped it. Instead I had allowed my mother to live in pain and die in pain. I visualised the moment when my grandfather had dragged Kaali away by her hair as I sat colouring, not affected by her abject fear. I wondered if he was still alive.

I was desperate to find out where Abha was and made mental lists of all the ways I could approach this search and the words I would utter when I finally confront him. I wanted revenge and that he should suffer at my hands. I wanted to thrust my knife into his body over and over again and hear him beg me for forgiveness.

CHAPTER 4

I had just finished doing my GCE 'O' levels and felt confident about my results and surprised everyone by being such a promising student. I was given permission at the age of sixteen to find a job. This was to be a temporary holiday job and I had assured Evie that I would go back to college to do my 'A' levels as she had high hopes for me.

Social services sent me to a local factory that made shampoo and other toiletries, I was disappointed but delighted to do any job that would give me my own personal income. Each morning I would clock in and each afternoon when the bell rang for the factory to close for the day, I would clock out and join the herd who were all eager to get back to their families and homes. My mundane role was to stand at a conveyer belt putting lids on shampoo bottles until my fingers blistered at the end of each day. The machinery was loud and the people were loud. Nobody really talked to me unless they had to but I did not care. I was just the little hard working hamster at the treadmill. But, at the end of my second week, I was in heaven when I received my first pay packet in a little brown envelope. I counted the notes and coins over and over again comparing them to my payslip. I bought a cake to take back to Evie and the others much to their delight. Life was pleasant without dramas and hate. This was what my mother had strived for and I did not want to disappoint her.

Charlie worked on the factory floor collecting the crates of packed shampoo bottles and transferring them to the storerooms on a trolley. He was eighteen years old, of slim build and a pleasant head of orange hair. He would walk in with a manly swagger pushing the trolley to collect the crates and wink at me as he passed. I liked him. He was funny and made me smile. Some of the other workers noticed and started to tease us.

"Watch it, Kari. Charlie's after you."

"Leave her alone, Charlie. She's too sweet and innocent for you."

I enjoyed the attention and enjoyed even more the attention I received from Charlie.

Evie noticed I was spending more time getting ready each morning, there wasn't much that she missed. She kindly offered to go shopping with me to have a 'girlie' day out, which I politely declined. I was no longer comfortable with getting intimate with anyone, especially with someone who saw themselves as my mother figure.

Friday afternoon came round slowly as I eagerly awaited the moment I collected my wage packet. I clocked out and was making my way to the gates when Charlie briskly walked up behind me.

"Hi, do you fancy coming out to see a film with me tonight, or even tomorrow?"

I felt a thrill but hesitantly replied, "No sorry, I can't!"

Charlie saw my struggle and misinterpreted my thoughts, "It's ok. I promise I'll behave".

He looked at me glancing sideways and winked, "Saturday night then? I'm a gentleman, I promise!"

After some resistance, I finally gave him my address and agreed that he collected me at seven the following evening.

Evie was extremely excited and nervous for me having a first date. I think it brought back memories of her early courting days and romantic times with Derek.

I was light-hearted and for the first time felt like a person without a past. Evie and Derek were quite anxious and quoted a list of acceptable behaviour from Charlie and coins for the phone booth if I wanted to be collected and brought back. Charlie was punctual and introduced himself and even told them where he lived assuring them that he would bring me back by ten. He was very polite and shook their hands, promising them once again that he would return me safely.

We did not talk much as we walked together side by side, keeping an arm's length distance between us and queued for the tickets. We were both nervous but there was a warm connection that did not need words. He placed his hand on my back to guide me to the seats, a warm touch that caressed and made me turn around and giggle at him. He gave me a peck on my nose which had us both laughing and we settled down hand in hand to watch an action packed Roger Moore film.

I was in a surreal world, walking on air. The temptation of losing the past and forgetting my focus would be to my regret and I would never be able to forgive myself for not avenging my mother's suffering or her death. So when Charlie took me back home and asked if would come out for a coffee the next day, my response was a flat "No".

"No? Why not?"

I'm sorry, I can't explain. It's complicating."

"Don't you like me?"

"Of course I do! But I have problems and first need to sort my life out."

"So if you didn't like me would you come out again?"

"Don't be silly. I'm sorry I shouldn't have come out today. I'm not a nice person. I'm sorry I can't"

Charlie was crestfallen and confused. I was definitely complicating but he was not going to give up easily and was prepared to pester me and find out more, but slowly and gently.

"What are these problems? I'm sure I can help! Can we still be friends and talk?" he asked cocking his head to one side.

"You don't want to know my problems! Yes, I'd like to still be friends. Honestly, I'm really sorry."

"It's okay. But as a friend I'm here if you ever want to talk or want any help."

I gave him a quick kiss on the cheek and ran indoors.

CHAPTER 5

Charlie took me to a football match for the first time to watch Derby County play. I was so excited and loved the roars and chanting from the crowds. He wrapped his black and white striped scarf around my neck to keep me warm as I would not let him wrap his arms around me or even hold my hand.

Charlie had been drinking cans of beer and I had drunk a couple of cans of cider and was feeling light headed as if I was floating on candy floss. We linked arms as we stumbled out of the gates laughing and singing, carried away in the euphoria of the moment.

It had been raining and the pavements glistened under the streetlights. The crowds gradually dispersed but we could still hear some rogue groups singing in the distance.

As we turned into a dark quiet street, Charlie nudged me against a wall and lifted my chin up with his free hand. His grey eyes were smiling, but glazed and slightly bloodshot with the alcohol running through his body.

"You're so pretty. I wish you'd just be my girlfriend."

"Don't, Charlie. I want to go home. I'm not interested."

"What's the matter with you? A little bit of kissing and cuddling isn't going to hurt!" he laughed teasingly.

"No!" I pulled away and marched off.

"Come on, baby. I'm crazy about you."

He grabbed me and pushed me against the wall.

"Let me go! Now! Or you will be sorry" I hissed, getting angry.

"Or what? Hey, baby! Or why will I be sorry?" he taunted.

He pressed his lips down on mine, stinking of beer and clumsily trying to nibble my lips.

"Get off!" I screamed and tried to push him away.

His grip on my arm was tight and he was breathing down my neck. The stench of his breath made me feel sick and triggered my subconscious disgust of men. With my free hand, I brandished my shiny blade from my inside pocket and held it at his throat. I swiped it gently just to draw a little blood, it was only a fine superficial line.

"What the fuck are you doing!? You want to slash my throat just 'cos I tried to kiss you!"

"I did warn you," I said still holding the knife at his throat.

Charlie looked at me in horror as he staggered back. I wet a tissue in a puddle to clean the blade before I smugly hid it back inside my inner pocket. I offered him a tissue to dab the slight bleed, smiling, not wanting to make a drama of such a small incident. He kept looking at me, walking away shaking his head in disbelief. I could not stop smiling. I had perversely enjoyed the moment and wished I had pushed the blade in a little deeper, not to kill but just to feel the power.

"I'm sorry!" I shouted, only slightly regretting my reaction to his drunken kiss, "I'm really sorry!"

"Well you don't need me to protect you. You'd better walk home yourself."

He turned around and marched off.

Evie and Derek were angry with Charlie when I arrived back alone, but I just ran past to my bedroom not wanting to give any explanation.

The next day, I refused to answer any questions from Evie about the sudden end of our friendship and I gave no further signs of being upset over it, so Charlie was no longer a topic of conversation. He often returned to my thoughts and I regretted pulling out my blade, but I wanted him to apologise for provoking me, as far as I was concerned he was to blame. I was no longer interested in being his friend and even less to be his girlfriend.

In the workplace, Charlie completely ignored me, which suited me fine rather than having to make pretentious small talk. I was a little sorry that our friendship was over, it had been fun. However, it was not the right time for romance or unproductive friendships.

Fortunately, my six-week contract had also come to an end and I was due to start back at college.

However, much to Evie's dismay, on my first day I refused to go and went to the job centre instead. I wanted to earn money, much more than the factory ever paid. I wanted a challenging job that was not demoralising and made me feel like a zombie each day.

I scanned the staff at the job centre to see which member seemed the most amenable.

A young girl walked up to me, "hello, Kari!"

I did not recognise her.

"It's Julie. I was at the Grange children's home with you."

I was the only tiny brown girl in the home, so it was hardly surprising that she recognised me. I now remembered her, but she had changed. She no longer looked mousy and dull. Julie was now a smartly dressed, well-manicured young woman.

"Come on, let's have a smoke outside and catch up."

I didn't smoke but we chatted for a little while and found out that we had both been fostered, but Julie, who was now eighteen, was working and renting a flat with friends. She said she often popped into the job centre always on the lookout for something better or a second small part-time job although she loved her current job.

She said she would speak to her boss to see if there were any vacancies, the pay was quite good. We agreed to meet the following afternoon outside a local café. I went back in to the job centre but Julie decided that she would go back home instead.

I was quite pleased as my outstanding exam results stood me in good stead for many job offers. I went away with employer addresses and application forms, some that offered a relatively attractive salary.

The process of doing job applications was extremely frustrating. I had no ambitions for a career, I just wanted to earn lots of money, travel to India and find Abha. I had been very prudent and spent hardly any of my money from the Hampshire's factory and had instead put it all into a Post Office savings account. I loved looking at my account book, seeing the savings grow each week.

CHAPTER 6

I met Julie at midday after posting the completed applications, it was a mundane task and I could see that my fortunes were not going to increase dramatically in the short term. But my choices were limited to the point that I was reluctant to even eat in a café and spend money unnecessarily. Julie offered to treat me to lunch or go back to her place where we could have a sandwich and coffee.

Curiosity led me back to her flat, which was on the second floor of a small, clean council estate compared to some of the filthier holes they called homes. All the flats had the outside walls painted cream and balconies overlooking a central green with a big notice 'No Ball Games'.

The inside of the flat was equally well maintained just like Julie and her flatmates. Neither were at work, but leant sloppily over of the balcony smoking some very sickly smelling roll ups. There were incensed candles and joss sticks flickering on side tables, attempting to disguise the scent of the illicit drugs. She introduced me to Debbie and Leila, both manicured and elegant like Julie. They looked like struggling models who were cynical of attention and eyed me suspiciously, not open or welcoming.

"It's ok, Kari and I were at the same children's home when we were young. She's job hunting." They just nodded and looked away seemingly uninterested but conscious and wary of my presence. Julie made small talk while she made cheese and pickle sandwiches and coffee. She talked about how her life was transformed and she no longer felt under pressure and was in full control of her destiny. She now had a close knit circle who she considered to be her only family and knew they would always be there for her. It felt good to belong and feel safe she added chirpily.

"So why aren't you at work today? Or your friends?" I asked not believing a word of her apparent sincerity.

"It's shift work and mostly evenings. That's why I love it, frees up our days to do whatever we want."

"So what do you do?"

"I'm a hostess. We're in the entertainment industry."

I already had my suspicions of the nature of her so called employment but carried on questioning her, giving the appearance of naivety.

"So you work in a club? But I'm not eighteen yet."

"Oh don't worry about that. Anything can be sorted. They give you a living and clothes allowance too. And my rent gets paid!"

"So what do you do in the club? And where is it?"

"It's not a club, we get a phone call to meet a client at a particular address, sometimes a hotel and sometimes their home and we just entertain them."

"Entertain? You mean you have sex with them. You work as a prostitute!"

"I'm not a prostitute." Julie retorted haughtily. "This is far classier and our clients have money. Look come to the bedroom, I'll show you my things."

She slammed back her chair and flounced towards her room, throwing open her wardrobe doors and jewellery boxes.

"Look! Look! Do you honestly think I could afford any of this or this flat if I did anything else or worked as some cheap prostitute?"

I looked at her disgusted. I would rather scrub the dirtiest toilets and earn less money than have constant sex with lecherous strangers and be the servile object of drunken, fat, old men.

"You're the fool! You think that just 'cos you kicked Baden in the balls and can handle a knife that you're better than anyone else", she retorted not liking the look of disdain in my face.

"I am better than you. I'm not some slimy man's toy. You're just an ignorant victim!"

I could not help myself being so forthright, maybe it was my own disappointment that I had expected a better opportunity and the revile I felt in anyone gifting themselves to a queue of men.

"How dare you! You are a pathetic snob who has nothing and no one! To think I was going to help you!" Julie slapped me hard across the face.

Adrenalin kicked in and I grabbed Julie by the hair and pulled her onto the bed holding my knife to the side of her neck.

"I don't care what you think of me! You're the bloody idiot who thinks you're in control of your life and safe with your prostituting family".

Julie's words had stung me that I had nothing and I had no one. It was the truth and all I wanted to do was push my blade deep into her throat. She looked wide-eyed and traumatised, screaming for me to stop. Debbie and Leila came running in and I quickly let go and backed away with my knife. Droplets of blood slid down onto the carpet and I had a passing glimpse of Charlie with that same expression of disbelief.

"She's okay, it's only a little nick. I'm not here to cause trouble. I'm not here to hurt anyone. I'm sorry, Julie!"

"Get out, you stupid bitch!" yelled Debbie, "We know people who'll put you in your place if you ever come back here again!" Julie sat up sobbing while Leila grabbed a towel and held it to the side of her neck hugging her and comforting her.

I pushed past Debbie, wiping my blade on the bedcovers as I passed and calmly left the room.

CHAPTER 7

I told Evie that I was going to London for the day by coach to meet up with Joan and Carol and left early next morning. It was my nature to always tell Evie and Derek my plans as opposed to asking them. It never occurred to me to ask them. I knew the limits and boundaries and if I chose to exceed them I did so in silence. Evie and especially Derek sensed my strong will and probably felt that I was wise enough not to resort to anything too drastic, so generally were quite happy just to be informed. They lightly questioned my travel plans and reeled out the standard safety warnings ensuring I had enough loose change to make a phone call in an emergency.

I liked sitting on the coach watching people getting on and off at each stop. I passed the hours on the motorway chasing the raindrops as they trickled down the window pane. I peered inside cars to conjure up stories for the drivers and their destinations. A young man was fleeing from the police after having assaulted his younger sister. A spectacled grey haired woman was driving to her father's funeral to make sure he was dead. My macabre thoughts made me smile but I doubted if others would appreciate my humour if they could have read my mind.

In my world these were real lives, not the cosy homes where emotions were numbed and cushioned. Real people had fire and passion in their hearts and dared to confront their fears. Real people suffered at the hands of their keepers. The cosy home provided by Evie was like a surreal film where every scene was predictable and repetitive. Its calming influence had not destroyed the evil seed of revenge that had long been planted in my soul, it reinforced the need to break out and to inflict pain once more.

In London, I made my way to Joan's house, noticing the changes. The roads I remembered as being wide, now seemed claustrophobically narrow. It all seemed much shabbier than when I lived here. It was probably the distortion of my childhood memories. There were more parked cars crowding the already stifled homes but the familiarity shed some warmth and I was eager to reach Joan's front door.

I would have been disappointed if Joan had moved house but it seemed unlikely. The front door was now painted a gay red, glossed and brightened up the shabby brickwork. I excitedly knocked on the shiny brass knocker. I had not actually written to her to say I was coming, so was hoping it would be a happy surprise and that she was actually at home.

A very aged and plump version of Joan finally opened the door. She looked at me in stunned disbelief and hugged me close, tears pricking her eyes and rolling down her cheeks. My heart was pounding at the unexpected emotion I felt. Joan had been good to my mother and to me. I knew she had tried hard to keep me by the sound of the letters that Carol had sent. She took my hand and limped towards the living room. We sat on the sofa and she buried her face in my hands sobbing.

"I thought of you every single day and I still think of you all the time. You are my sweet flower. They broke my heart when they took you away, so far away. Please forgive me, I really tried to keep you, I really tried!"

We hugged and I held her tight.

"And your poor mother, I should never have left her alone, my poor Kaali," Joan wept uncontrollably as I sat moved by the depth of her guilt but not blaming her for any of those desperate days.

Her tears finally subsided and she began to update me on their life and some of the neighbours. She told me that Carol was at college and would not be home until after four, I wasn't sure if I could stay that long as it was still only eleven in the morning and had plenty to attend to.

I told her my exam results and she was thrilled and said that it was with my influence that Carol had achieved so much at school. She made me promise that I would return to education and create a career for myself. I tentatively asked about Abha and his whereabouts. Joan nodded knowingly, she had been keeping documents and newspaper cuttings and following the case as much as she could. She brought out a large carrier bag with lots of labelled brown envelopes.

"This is for you, I knew you would come back one day and ask questions. I hope it helps you to find out more about what happened to your mother. It's the least I could do. And, Kari, your mother was cremated. There was nobody else at the funeral, only Carol and me. I still have her ashes safely for you if you want them. If not I can scatter them, or we can do it together. Whatever you want."

Joan was like my mother come down from heaven. It was now my turn to burst out crying releasing all the sadness and frustration knotted up for so long. Again we held each other close, remembering the terrible past and the vision of my mother on death's bed.

Joan gently pulled away, "Let me get you some tea and food. Some nice coronation chicken sandwiches. I know how much you loved those."

I now found myself laughing hysterically, it truly felt like coming home.

I pulled out all the various envelopes which contained newspaper cuttings, letters from the coroner, police statements and finally the death certificate.

The cause of death was recorded as 'punctured lungs due to trauma'.

The cuttings related to small items about an abusive husband who had now vanished. There was a photograph of him as a wanted man and various sites of where he had been last seen. These were all dated almost ten years ago now and nothing recent had been published. Many people had phoned the police about sightings but all proved to be a false trail of mistaken identity or vengeance to expel foreigner neighbours.

Abha had vanished and the police had no further leads, hence it appeared the chase had been buried into their portfolio of unsolved cases.

Joan brought in a tray with sandwiches and tea. Also on the tray was a small black and gold tea caddy, elegant and delicate in design. I knew instantly that these were my mother's ashes. There was no ceremony as she handed me the tin, cupping it with both her hands. I took it gratefully and placed it carefully in my bag. It felt strange to be reunited with my mother in quite a matter of fact way.

I expressed my sorrow that I could not stay to meet Carol but I had other errands and promised Joan that I would keep in touch. Joan hugged me and made me promise once again that I would write and visit whenever I could.

I left feeling light hearted and positive and even more eager to find Abha.

CHAPTER 8

I took a bus into central London and made my way to the India Tea Centre. I lingered outside the large shop windows feeling a little too conspicuous and self-conscious to walk in. It looked surprisingly elegant inside with equally elegant customers. I had not realised that Abha had worked in what appeared to be such a prestigious establishment. The staff preened themselves in front of their clientele with their starched white uniforms. I had never seen Abha in his uniform or seen my mother ever having to wash or iron it. I would have liked to have had sight of a smart, well-spoken father rather than the arrogant, foul mouthed man that returned home every day.

Finally, with some determination, I walked in towards the cashier and asked to see the manager.

"I'm afraid we have no vacancies, dear" said the cashier very pleasantly and politely.

"I'm not after a job right now. I'm looking for my father."

The cashier eyed me, puzzled, "Father? Who is your father?"

"Abha Chetti".

"Oh! Oh my goodness! He doesn't work here anymore. Such a long time ago! The manager is new here, he won't have met your father."

He looked at me puzzled, "You don't know where your father is?"

I looked back sadly, "No, I don't have anyone else, I haven't seen my father for about ten years now".

"Wait, I know who might be able to help you. It was a very sad time for him when his son died. I did not know that he had a daughter as well".

The cashier, phoned through to the kitchen and whispered something in Hindu.

"Follow me", he said kindly and led me to the staff area, "I really did not know he had a daughter!"

He asked me to wait at the inner doors and the chef, Shakeel, would be along soon.

Shakeel appeared to be a friendly, warm man, who looked at me with sorrow. But I was not fooled, he would have been just as capable of going home each day and beating his wife and daughters.

"So you are Abha's daughter. We all loved him very much, but he changed after his son died."

I could sense that he also had not known about my existence and was guarded as how he phrased each sentence.

"You really don't know where your father is?"

I shook my head sadly, "I really want to find him. He is the only family I have."

"I was in touch with him for some time after he left us. He was very sad and depressed. He stayed with some of my friends in Scotland and then went on holiday to India. I heard that he went because his mother was not well."

The information was useless. I needed a concrete lead to follow.

"Can I contact your friends in Scotland to see if they know anything?"

He reluctantly wrote the name, address and telephone number of his contact in Aberdeen.

"You should contact India first, I'm sure he must be there with his family. I hope he has found some peace and happiness. I don't understand why you don't know any of this?"

"Life has been complicating," I shrugged.

I thanked him for his help, always puzzled when I hear of Abha in a different light. That was the father who had been on the ship with us on an incredible journey. Why had he treated my mother with such utter disdain and refused to acknowledge my existence. If he had stood in front of me right then, I would have had no hesitation in ending his life, slowly and painfully, for every day that my mother had to live in relentless pain and anguish.

I phoned the Aberdeen number, but got a long singular monotone of a disconnected past. I vented my frustration by pathetically swearing down the phone. I wanted to scream for not having known the father that others had the privilege of knowing and that he would be so ashamed of me that he had not even acknowledged my existence to his colleagues. I took out my knife and hacked up the telephone cord systematically into several pieces.

An old man waited outside the phone booth, peering in through the pane. He looked down at me suspiciously as I barged past shouting, "It doesn't work! Someone's vandalised it!"

He jumped back startled as I slammed the booth door shut. I was in no mood for politeness and pleasantries.

Back on the coach, I knew I needed to make money. I couldn't see the point of going to Scotland and the only way forward would be to get back to Abha's roots and get back to India. Julie's offer was an unsavoury option but I had burned that bridge already and it was unlikely that she would trust me or entertain me. But the earnings capacity was a temptation.

Waiting for job application responses would be tedious and nothing was guaranteed. The money would be slow and the life mundane. My mind kept rotating back to Julie, If I could ensure that I stayed in control and wasn't just a pawn in the game, I could perhaps endure the so called entertainment industry for a short time. My skin prickled at the thought of the disgust and danger I would be opening myself up to.

It would be good to move out of Evie's cosy nest as it was beginning to stifle me. With all her good intentions, life was colourless and offered no inspiration, challenges or ambition. I, or the other children were never reprimanded or reproached for any reason. It was meaningful, tedious conversations to put things right and Derek may as well have been made out of marshmallow. If I had screamed and jumped through the window, I'm sure Evie would just have said, "Don't worry about the window, dear. Is there anything you want to talk about?"

There was no pressure or firm hand to lay down the limits. I should have thrived and allowed the goodness to wash over me, but I knew too much about the minds of men. They would not be my saviour and I would be my champion. I wanted to leap out of bed each morning knowing that I controlled my day and my destiny, instead of the futile conversations of petty cash and laundry. I had to take a leap of faith to accelerate the journey to my goal.

CHAPTER 9

The thought of any man touching me was abhorrent. However, the idea that I could dominate men and inflict pain upon them, excited me. I did not consider myself to be a freak, I merely wanted to see the vulgarity of the male ego to be reduced to a snivelling wreak.

I regretted threatening Julie and knew that had been an automatic reaction, just like my foolish reaction to Charlie's amorous advances. But it angered me that she could let any man maul her for his own gratification just so that she had a nice wardrobe and flat. She was owned and whether she realised it or not and I was unable to suppress my disgust.

I returned to Julie's flat, mellowed and unthreatening to find all three girls confronting me at the doorway, barricading my entrance with threats and snarls.

"Julie, I'm truly sorry. I made a big mistake. It's automatic with me whenever I feel threatened. You know what it was like in the home, I don't mean to judge you. Please give me another chance."

"We girls stick together and trust each other. We don't trust you."

"You can trust me, I promise. Please help me. Please! Please!"

Julie looked me over warily.

"If you step out of line that means you've probably killed me off too. Hope you realise that."

Debbie and Leila walked away telling Julie that she was a fool to even consider including me.

"She'll get us all killed! You're an idiot to even consider!"

Julie sighed, looked straight at me, "Martha, our boss, won't stand for any nonsense. You might want to go away and think it over again. It probably isn't your cup of tea!"

"I've already thought about it. It's not my cup of tea and that's an understatement! But I need money and need lots quickly!"

"Ok then, I first need to make a phone call and then we can go straight over."

We walked along the main Northampton road for over ten minutes and then turned into an alley between a newsagents and bookmakers. We climbed up to the second floor on spiral iron steps that seemed more like a fire escape. Julie knocked on the door which had no number.

A middle aged motherly frame let us in.

"Hello, pet. How are you? So you've brought your exotic friend along. It's good to have variety."

Her words made me feel quite sick, but I supressed my icy retort. I would play the game my way and be out of it within six months.

"I've just made some rock cakes. Put the kettle on, Julie dear."

The cosy set up to put me at ease was obvious and deliberate.

"Where do you live, dear? We have a lovely new flat empty not too far from the town centre. You'd love it!"

We sat around the kitchen table eating cakes and drinking tea. It was like a visit to your favourite grandmother.

"We have a lovely doctor who keeps check on all my darling girls. Don't want you getting sick now do we?"

Julie nodded, "yes, Brian is really nice, he does an initial medical check-up and if you have any problems you can always go to him anytime."

Martha smiled affectionately at Julie and chose her words very carefully, "my favourite girl! Wish they were all as intelligent and beautiful as you".

"I tell you what, here's the address and the keys to the new flat. I'll give you some cash for the cab and if you both like it, you can move in together."

It seemed like the interview was already over and I had the job, refusing was probably not an option at this stage.

"Julie can be your partner in crime so to speak!" laughed Martha. "We'll sort out all the silly details, money and all that, in a couple of days."

Martha was beaming, chuckling as she saw us to the door, "just pop round anytime if you want a chat or advice. I'm always here for my girls!"

"She really is very nice as long as you stick to the rules," explained Julie as we carefully wormed our way down the fire escape.

I made no comment as my only thoughts were on how I was going to deal with this in a detached manner without losing my sanity.

CHAPTER 10

"Evie, I've got a job at the bookmakers, but strictly I'm under age." I walked in cheerfully with Julie tagging along.

Evie frowned, "I don't like the sound of that. Definitely not a good idea and Social Services will have you back in a home if you're not careful."

"Pleas, Evie, listen! It's because I'm good with numbers, I'll be working in the office out the back. No one sees me. This way I can go to college in the day." The lies flowed like honey on a summer's day. I knew the last part would keep Evie happy. I also introduced Julie to her and assured her that I would sometimes stay at her flat if it got too late.

Julie appeared like a reasonable, sensible adult, "Don't worry Mrs Foster, the manageress is really kind. I've worked with her for some years now. We really are a good team!"

Evie knew that if Social Services got to know any of this, there would be problems not just for me but also for herself and Derek. She looked trustingly at Julie and nervous about refusing. She acknowledged my independent streak and my impatience to spread my wings and leave the nest.

From that day on I more or less came and went as I pleased with no questions asked and no more fabrications of the hideous truth.

I loved being in my new flat and having an allowance to decorate my room and pamper myself. I was under no illusions of the penalty I had to pay and made preparations for the job on hand.

My room became a cloud of soft pink, a replica of Carol's, probably far too childish now but it made my heart smile. However, my new wardrobe was predominantly black right down to my lipstick. I was determined to be the mistress at every meeting and not cower beneath any man. I was the hunter and he would be my prey.

I had a fleeting health check from Brian and was given six month's supply of the contraceptive pill. His make shift surgery consisted of a bed and a cabinet full of pills at the corner of his living room, on a floor below Martha. He questioned me in slurred incoherent tones induced by alcohol, "Any health problems? No? Excellent!"

So much for Julie's recommendations but I would have been foolish to expect anything more. The phone call for my first client had me convulsing in the bathroom at what lay ahead. Julie comforted me and assured me it would get easier after the first time. I sensed her guilt at having lured me into her wretched lifestyle. She wanted to help me get ready, but I refused. I needed my own space and had my own plans.

I struggled into a tight fitting black dress, which compressed my already small mounds of breast. I jabbed scissors into my hair to look unruly and unkempt and with gelled fingers spiked out the short strands in all directions. I had no intention of looking groomed or glamorous.

My heavy eyelids were smothered in grey eyeshadow to make me look almost skeletal. Thick dark false eyelashes veiled the disgust I had for myself. I found an elegant pair of silver earrings, each dangled like a glistening blade.

I put on thick black stockings and thigh high boots. I had inserted pockets on the inside of each boot and slowly eased into each a flick knife and a thin blade.

I was proud that I had budgeted my allowance well and made some excellent purchases, placing the rest into my savings account.

Finally, I shrouded my entire body with a sparkling black chiffon shawl like the night with a thousand stars.

I saw the waiting car from my window and made my way to the door.

Julie looked aghast, "Oh my God!! You look like an evil witch going to a funeral! Martha will go crazy and I'll get the blame!!"

"Julie, stop it! I know what I'm doing. There'll be no complaints."

I went to work feeling strong and confident almost relishing the challenge and wanting to draw blood.

CHAPTER 11

The hotel was about twenty minutes' drive away. It's dark, gloomy location suited my witchlike attire. There was still an exquisite beauty in the scene, like a temptress' castle in the mist, romantic but dangerous.

The doormen opened the arched double doors and did not flinch as I walked through cautiously. No one raised their heads, no one had any intention of making eye contact. They were all far too busy making themselves as invisible as possible. I went towards the grey, marbled, ornate reception desk and asked for room four. The clerk pointed me in the direction with his well-manicured hands, without lifting his head.

It felt as if people were living in the shadows of an alternate, dark underworld.

I walked stealthily in my weaponed boots, wincing inwardly with the discomfort, along the corridor and tapped coyly on the door. The pounding in my heart, the vibrating in my ears, the throbbing in my head, I held onto the door frame to steady myself. My breath was rising and falling at the wretchedness and humiliation of the task that lay before me.

The door opened a crack and I was allowed in by a tall middle aged woman with long chestnut braids down her back. She seemed much too old for her hair although her grooming was immaculate. Her alabaster skin with its layers of foundation barely cracked when she attempted a smile.

I looked around puzzled. There was no man in sight.

"What's your name?" she asked in a soothing, husky voice.

"Katie" I replied promptly.

"No, your real name?"

"Katie" I repeated.

"I must say, you're dressed very strangely. But it suits you."

I remained standing, confused and at a loss at what happens next.

"Just relax, Katie. Wish you would do something about that dumb expression on your face." She laughed out aloud obviously enjoying my naïve confusion and open reaction.

"Call me Eva. This evening you follow orders because I am paying!" she declared firmly.

I nodded getting to grips with my totally unexpected dilemma but felt secure with my knives caressing my thighs.

"What would you like to eat? The risotto sounds good or would you prefer something spicier?"

I did not trust anyone's curry except my mother's, "risotto," I replied.

"Sit down and relax" said Eva beckoning me to the sofa. She phoned room service and ordered risotto, salads, bread rolls followed by chocolate cheesecake along with two bottles of champagne. She handed me a glass of wine while we waited.

"I like to eat well and enjoy my evenings. I don't believe in quick sex and then throw you out the door." She used a matter of fact tone and asserted her control.

"How old are you?"

"Eighteen".

"Do you ever utter more than one word at a time?"

"Yes".

Once again Eva burst out laughing, "You really are a breath of fresh air. I can see that you're obviously in shock, your first time? Yes?"

I nodded and let out a sigh. I sipped my wine cautiously, unwilling to let it loosen my tongue or impair my reactions.

Eva, nonplussed, carried on chattering, reminding me of a more vivacious and twisted version of Joan. I was becoming more relaxed against my better judgement but intent on staying alert. I picked at the bland risotto but munched on the bread hoping that it would absorb the alcohol. I could feel my senses already leaving me as Eva fed me with morsels of the cheesecake and carefully wiped away the chocolate from my lips.

"You have such a sweet face. It's sad that I have to share you with others."

I was now feeling very dizzy and disorientated. Eva held my hand and led me towards the bed, she may as well have led me to the gates of hell.

She removed my shawl and let it drop to the floor and guided me to sit on the edge of the bed.

She unzipped my boots, removing each carefully and fortunately made no remark of any hidden knives. She eased me onto the bed, all the while whispering in my ear and caressing me. I wished I had drunk even more so that I would have been oblivious to the tampering of my body. But I played the game well which seemed to go on for an eternity. There was no pleasure, just disgust. It did not matter whether it was a man or a woman, it just felt so wrong. But I did get paid, I got paid well, additional to anything Martha would already have received.

"This is extra for you my sweets, just to tempt you for a return visit", said Eva as she pressed a roll of bank notes into my childish bosom. She helped me into the back of the cab and I was returned to my flat by midnight.

Even in my drunken stupor, I walked straight into the shower, falling down as I struggled to take off my clothes. I sat naked, angry with the world and finally understanding why my mother could never stop washing and never felt clean. I too felt dirty and diseased. I felt angry with myself, wishing I had shredded her aged skin from her scrawny face. I convinced myself that I was in control and had walked away intact and richer. There was no doubt, I had to go through this sordid process again and again.

CHAPTER 12

The next afternoon, Martha walked into the flat, there was no need to knock, she always carried with her a large bunch of keys. Julie, lying on the sofa watching TV, jumped to her feet.

"Martha!"

"Where's Kari? Is she all right?"

"She's still in bed, hangover I presume, but she seems alright," said Julie still in shock at Martha's surprise visit.

Julie had tried to get me up earlier to talk about the previous evening but my sore head refused to respond. It was now past midday and I felt ill, saturated with alcohol and anxiety. Martha came into my room, gently knocking the door first and placed the back of her hand on my forehead.

"I shall warn that client not to ply you with so much alcohol. It is not acceptable."

Martha grumbled away like an anxious mother and went to the kitchen, pulling out of her checked, plastic shopping bag, bread, eggs, bacon, mushrooms, the full works. She proceeded to cook a good solid brunch to feed an army. She laid a tray with the plated meal, orange juice and coffee and brought it back to my room. She had only prepared one plate much to the fury of Julie.

Martha got me to sit up and placed the tray on my lap, soothing me and coaxing me to eat. I wallowed in the attention, grateful for the solid food.

Julie leaned against the doorway watching with jealousy and resentment. She had never been privy to such royal treatment, even when she had been bruised or beaten by a client although Martha had always told her that she was her favourite girl.

"My poor Kari," Martha cooed. "My client had a lot of good things to say about you. I hope she didn't hurt you at all?"

I shook my head, how would I explain to Martha that my pain was not going to be eased by breakfast and aspirins. Although it was highly unlikely that she would care as long as the clients returned and the money poured in.

I focused on the welcome tray of food and coffee. My head was still pounding but my thoughts were no longer clouded.

"Did she give you an extra tip?"

"It's in my bag" I said pointing to the bag thrown in the corner. "I didn't count it."

Martha snapped her fingers at Julie to bring her the bag. Inside was the roll of banknotes. After counting, Martha replaced the notes and said kindly, "You keep this my dear. You deserve it. Next time we'll share."

"Thank you, Martha" I said sweetly, playing the charade.

"Now you stay in bed and take it easy today. I must take care of my golden girl."

As she walked past Julie she muttered, "For goodness sake, sort yourself out! You look like a tired office clerk!"

Julie was stunned. She always made an effort and had still not received the bonus she was promised for finding me. It had been her ploy to hang around job centres and seek out potential victims or employees as she liked to call them.

She stood by my bed with arms folded, "I just can't believe this! You go out dressed like the angel of death and now you're the golden girl!"

"Stop shouting, Julie. I have a headache! Anyway, I'm only doing this for another month".

"Don't be ridiculous! You can't leave. If you try, you'll either be maimed or dead!"

"So be it. Both of those options would be better than this!"

"She has some bully boys who enjoy their job. I've seen girls after they've paid a visit. It really is nasty stuff."

"I've made up my mind." I staggered out of bed and carried the empty tray through the kitchen and calmly proceeded to wash the dishes and tidy up, partly out of habit and it was therapy to do something normal.

"You're mad! What about me, they'll beat me up if they think I helped you."

I made no comment. Julie was more than capable of looking after herself. If she chose to be the victim, as far as I was concerned, that was her choice.

I showered once again and muddled through my thoughts as to my next step. My hair was a disaster and I looked like a flea infested rat.

Julie looked at me shaking her head said with disdain, "You look ugly! To think Martha wants me to follow your style! No thank you!"

Julie went to her room, slamming every door on the way.

The rest of the month was probably the worst of my life but I got bolder with each meeting. I even brandished my knives to flaunt my expertise and delicately drew some blood. The men were thrilled, terrified and loved the dominance. I realised how pathetic and stupid the minds of men could be. I relished the day when I would draw blood from Abha.

The balance in my savings book had been growing pleasantly, far more than I had anticipated. It was tempting to stay in the trade but I was not greedy, I had a purpose. I packed a few basic items and quietly left to return to Evie, popping into the bank on the way to deposit the last of my earnings.

The truth of my employment, massaged in my favour, was related back to the horrified Fosters.

They were adamant that both the Social Services and the police had to be involved. Evie felt guilty that they had not been more assertive and had failed in their duty of care towards me. Derek made phone calls while Evie sat me in front of the hall mirror and cocooned me in a large bath towel, while she snipped away at my hair. When she had finished, I looked like a little pixie from my far away fairy tales. All that was missing were the pointed ears. I loved my new look. I gave Evie a hug and went to have a long soak in the bath.

The rest of the day was exhausting with visits from welfare workers, police and doctors. I gave as much information as possible, although I realised that I only had first names and no addresses other than the flat that I had been living in and Martha's flat.

There was concern for my safety from Martha and her gang and I was moved to a safe house in Birmingham, where I had been whisked away the same night. Although I was used to the continuous transfers, I did feel a twinge of sadness to leave Evie. It was the closest thing that I had experienced to a stable family home. Events and phases of my life passed by frantically as if I was viciously tearing pages from a horror book, looking for that glimmer of hope or the happy fairy tale ending.

There were are moments of peace and smiles. Mostly my young life had been about insecurity and fear. I was nearly eighteen and dreading my legal independence. Nobody would be obliged to look out for me any longer and there would be no safety net or anyone to turn to. I lay listless with my back to the horrid world.

CHAPTER 13

Raj and Najma knocked and walked in with a tray.

"It's been three days now, Kari. Please eat and drink a little", begged Raj.

"Auntie is worried that you will get too weak and end up in hospital", added Najma.

"It's your birthday soon, we should get out, the three of us and have a meal somewhere".

"Auntie is baking a cake for you".

"No to everything" I said flatly.

Raj was irritated, "So you want to lie in bed and die! We can't read your mind! You have to talk or nobody can help you!"

How could I tell these relatively naïve girls that all I wanted to do was to take revenge for my mother's death. I wanted to stop at nothing. How my evil mind plotted and schemed to hurt everyone who had crossed our paths. How I had used my knives more often than necessary and enjoyed inflicting pain on others.

Raj was in hiding after having run away from home to escape from being sent to India for an arranged marriage. Najma was also in protective custody after her now imprisoned father had killed her English boyfriend with much collusion from other members of her family.

Everyone seemed to be running and hiding. Nobody was free especially if you were an Asian girl. The girls did not know my history and I was not sure how much our 'auntie' knew.

I willed myself to turn around and face the sweet girls.

"I don't want to be eighteen! I don't want to grow up."

Raj looked at me sadly. Considering they were both younger than me, I still felt as if they were the older siblings who felt duty bound to protect me.

"I'm going to India on holiday and meet up with my mother's family."

"Are you mad!" yelled Najma, "They'll have you married off in a jiffy to a fat, bald second cousin, just to get him into the UK!"

I started laughing, "Don't be ridiculous! I have other plans".

"Come on, let's go down and have lunch with auntie. She has been really kind looking after us. We can talk about your plans when you've eaten something", said Raj

"I'm guessing that she's not really your auntie and are you two related?"

"We call everybody auntie. It's just the way it is. Naj and I have become close although we've only known each other for a week."

"We do have families and I guess that at some point we will be sent back. I'm actually dreading it but I do miss my sister. I hope she's okay" added Najma despondently.

"Okay then, let's go down!" I chirped, forcing a cheeriness to my voice and swinging my skinny legs off the bed.

We trooped downstairs carrying the tray to find Mrs Khan busy with a stack of letters. She smiled kindly at the sight of us, "come, girls, let's have lunch" and led us through to the kitchen table.

The aroma and taste brought back memories of my mother and I wished that she had been sitting next to me to enjoy this meal.

I regretted not having told her how much I loved her cooking. Somehow, she always mange to conjure up a meal from whatever scraps Abha reluctantly brought home. He would curse her stupidity and inability but in fact was envious of her resourcefulness and quiet capability.

Mrs Yasmin Khan was a strong minded woman who had lived in this country for many years and had escaped an abusive husband and his abusive family. After getting back on her feet, finding a job in Social Services, doing voluntary work to help other women who were in dire situations, she had turned to help the younger generation who were now at the mercy of the elders. Unwanted marriages were still being arranged, young girls were being sent on holiday to India, Pakistan and other Asian countries and never returned and there was a lot of emotional blackmail and pressure to conform to their age old traditions.

She received many insults and threats from people who accused her of breaking up families and being too influenced by the bad habits of the Westerners.

Mrs Khan was stoic in her attitude to all who reproached her and did not waiver in her efforts to shelter those at risk.

She had a profound effect on my outlook. I could see that she still had respect and embraced her culture and traditions, but was wise enough to see that the younger generation, especially girls, could not be expected to live in the West with a blinkered vision. We were not second class citizens who were incapable of making important decisions that had a huge impact on our lives. We were not born to merely please the elders.

She had daily chats with each of us in private to give us the opportunity to express our worries and fears. She never dismissed anything I said as being pointless or unachievable, but would ask me to consider what I thought were the pros and cons of any decision.

We did have ground rules, predominantly for our own safety, as the network of extended families were always on the lookout for familiar faces in hiding. This was more of an issue for Najma and Raj as my situation was completely different. I chose not to tell the girls of my reasons for being there, partly embarrassment and partly to protect them from the darker side of life.

It was my birthday and Mrs Khan baked a simple cake and the girls and I had fun icing it. I realised it was the first time that a birthday cake had ever been baked for me. They hugged me and shed tears when I told them this. It was such a simple thing; it was all that was needed to make the day very special.

They then made me sit and watch the longest Hindi movie ever, they all cried and shrieked at the never ending plot while I lay my head on Mrs Khan's lap and fell into a contented sleep.

The next morning, I awoke feeling strangely older and wiser. I felt blessed that in my life there had been some powerful and loving women, starting with my mother, then Joan, Evie and now Mrs Khan. I still could not banish the burning hate I felt for Abha and knew that until I could stand before him and thrust his guilt into his cowardly frame, I could never be at peace.

I told Mrs Khan that I wanted to get my passport sorted and take a trip to Madras as soon as possible. I showed her my savings book, containing the illicit earnings, to assure her that I was able to afford the plane ticket and that I would stay with my mother's family. I wrote to Indira, a short letter saying that I would be coming and wanted to scatter my mother's ashes in the river Krishna.

Raj and Najma were anxious when I told them my plans and made me promise that I would write to them from India and get back in touch when I returned. I promised knowing full well that it was superficial conversation.

Mrs Khan intuitively knew that my intentions ran much deeper than just wanting to get back to my mother's roots but did not question me further. She gave me one of her small old suitcases with little gifts to help me on my travels. There were tablets of soap with flannels, a fan, a purse filled with Indian rupees and coins left from her previous trips.

I was adamant that I would only be wearing jeans and T-shirts and none of the colourful garments offered by Raj and Najma. My hair had grown a little but still only reached the nape of my neck. On impulse I went to the hairdressers and got my hair dyed blue much to the horror of the girls. I felt compelled to be as far away as possible from the timid culture that they represented.

The next day I returned having got a tattoo of a snake from behind my ear to the front of my shoulder. It had been a painful experience and I still stung from the needle but it added to my resolve not to conform. Mrs Khan and the girls gave up saying anything and let me express my rebellious nature and vent my inner anger.

I took great care in hiding my knives and blades, behind cupboards, under floorboards and buried some in the garden, wrapped in plastic. I did not want to jeopardise my trip by carrying knives and taking foolish risks. I was confident that I could arm myself with any weapon very easily in India. I just kept back one blade, my favourite, which was thin and sleek like a shortened tomato knife to protect me for the rest of the week before I began my journey.

CHAPTER 14

We were woken up early next morning to the shattering of glass. A brick had been thrown through the living room window. Another brick followed shortly after through the kitchen window. Mrs Khan, an early riser, ran to find a scruffy, bearded man leaning against the lamppost outside her house. He spat on the ground as he saw her. He was joined by two youths, jeering and laughing, and the three men walked casually away. She suspected that the relatives of either Raj or Najma had somehow found out their hiding place. The girls started crying much to my irritation. I stormed out the front door yelling abuse at the men, while Mrs Khan begged me to get back indoors. I picked up a large stone and flung it at them, it clipped the side of one of the youth's face. He turned round and snarled but the older man dragged him away.

She hastily phoned the police and Social Services. The police arrived several hours later, smart, professional and very unhelpful. They were reluctant to get involved in what they ignorantly considered to be cultural family squabbles. However, they were concerned for her safety and advised her to install more secure locks. It was not just racial tension within the community but tension within the races that was a problem.

Social services arrived in the evening to discuss the future of us girls. I refused to move as I was now over eighteen and would be going to India shortly. They talked at length with Raj and Najma with a view to moving them to another safe house. However, Raj was now considering returning to her family. She missed them and was tired of hiding, she thought she would just get on with it and live the life that was expected of her. There was too much upheaval and uncertainty for her current existence. She had seen her cousins and friends married off reluctantly, but they mostly seemed to be happy and uncomplaining. Mrs Khan did not place any pressure on Raj but asked her to consider carefully before she made any decision, as how her return would be treated was unpredictable. But Raj was drawn back to her family, the umbilical pull was growing stronger and she wanted to phone her mother, the guilt she felt on running away was too much to bear. She was taken back home that same evening.

Najma on the other hand, whose situation was far more precarious, feared for her life from her brothers and uncles. She did not expect a welcome home from her mother, since her father had been imprisoned because of her, in fact the happy lives of the whole family had been turned upside down because of her. So alternative accommodation was found for her. She was taken away the next morning and nothing more was heard from her.

Mrs Khan and I lived together for another week until my flight to India. We had daily attacks of bricks and stones flung at the house. Most of the windows were boarded up and the back door was now barricaded. Parcels of excrement were posted through her letter box and men urinated on her walls in the night. All manner of waste was flung into her front and back gardens, including dead animals and used condoms. Local Asian shopkeepers would turn their back on her or fling down any change or goods on to the counter. Her tenacious traits weakened until sadly she could take no more.

She was moved by Social Services on the same day that I was due to fly out. I was relieved as I could not bear to think of her being persecuted alone.

I could not imagine how I was going to travel across India, and had listened intently to advice from Mrs Khan. Finally, packed and ready, I had hugged and kissed her and made my way to the bus station to catch the coach to the airport. I sat daydreaming of a life that could have been. I would be sitting high on my father's shoulders waving to my grandmother as we left the port. I would be back in time in Carol's room, being a child, reading fairy stories and dressing up as the fairy Queen, swishing my magic wand and putting the world to rights. I would have long flowing hair and walk hand in hand with Charlie along the river banks, we would be laughing and kissing then feeding each other little morsels from our picnic basket. I would be on the stage at university in my hat and gown, collecting my prize while my mother would be clapping wildly from the audience.

But in reality I was crossing the ocean to take revenge and commit murder.

I remembered scenes at my grandmother's kitchen, the fun times with my uncles, the teasing and the toys. I remembered the grating voice of Devi as she continued with a monotone of all the chores that needed attending to my mother. I could hear her softened tones whispered in my ear telling me what a sweet child I was and what a good hard working mother I had. I wanted to see my grandmother and hopefully she would open the door to Abha. I had no plans of what I would do or how I would do it. I just knew the outcome I desperately wanted.

My first stop would be to find Indira and scatter my mother's ashes, although she and the rest of the family had turned their back on my mother. It would not be an emotional bond as she had only contacted my mother for money, but it was a starting point.

CHAPTER 15

It was a very hot day in May when I landed at Madras airport. It was a modern western structure with a distinct Indian chaos. It was colourful and noisy. I felt like an ant looking for the exit. The many curious stares I received with my blue spiky hair and deadly tattoo made me feel strong and in control. I refused to be timid and subservient. As I stepped out of the airport, the oppressive heat, which was at almost forty degrees, seemed to burn a hole through my back. Nothing was familiar, I could not read any of the signs that appeared to be in either Hindi or Tamil. It was very dusty and a stench lurked in the air. It was strange to be surrounded by so many brown faces although mine was probably darker than most. Everyone looked small and sweaty and very poor. I was very protective of my belt which held my passport and some of my money, although I had money hidden in several places.

There was a rows of taxis. I went to the first one and showed Indira's address. The driver spoke in a very fast Tamil dialect and I made out that he may have said something ridiculous like five hundred rupees. I walked to the next driver who shouted in English, "No! No! Too far! Too far!"

Everyone seemed to repeat everything twice while shaking their heads. I wandered about asking various people who looked as if they may speak a little English when a young boy approached me smiling.

"You are lost?"

I was relieved to hear English although with a heavy Indian accent, which was not unpleasant. He sounded innocent and naïve and looked about sixteen.

"Hello, yes I'm lost. I'm trying to find the best way to reach this address."

He gave me a beaming smile, "we have to catch a taxi into town and then a train, and it's a long way."

"We? If you just tell me which stations I need to get on and off, I can manage."

"It is not safe to travel on your own. Young girls go missing all the time!"

"I'm more than capable of looking after myself. I only have a little money; I can't buy your ticket as well!" I was not prepared to spend more money than necessary.

"How old are you anyway, shouldn't you be at school or something!"

"My name is Max and I am twenty-three years old! You look like twelve!" he laughed but looked quite peeved. "I am not after your money, I am not going to rob you", he carried on indignantly. "I was just being nice and helpful because you were lost!"

I looked at him intently, deciding whether I should trust him or not.

"Where can I buy a good dagger or knife?" I asked sharply.

"Oh my goodness! You now want to kill me?"

"It's a present for my father".

"What about a present for your mother?"

"My mother is dead. She's in my bag", I said getting irritated and just wanted to be on my way.

Max looked at me curiously, "okay, I will take you to the market. We have to take the taxi into town first."

I was not sure that in the sweltering heat that I could manage the journey on my own, so reluctantly agreed, fiercely refusing help to carry my bags.

The taxi took us into the town centre and he negotiated the fare.

"The market is about ten minutes' walk, the driver would have charged you more if we hadn't stopped here."

Max stopped at a stall and bought a bottle of water for me. I accepted it gratefully but still keeping my guard.

Finally, after what seemed more like thirty minutes with my constant childlike pestering of 'are we nearly there?' we finally turned a corner where there was a street market offering all kinds of cheap plastic goods, vegetables and some more exotic items to tempt the tourists.

Max took me to the perfect stall where displayed were the most amazing bejewelled daggers and knives in all shapes and sizes. For my own pleasure, I would have bought several but resisted the temptation. I opted for a simple black handled blade.

It was elegant with a shiny ebony handle and the smooth blade promised a clean cut. In my excitement, I also went for a much larger weapon that was a cross between a dagger and a sword. It was long enough to cause serious damage but short enough to attach the sheath to my belt.

Max took over the bargaining and the weapons were bought.

"The station is just five minutes away"

I did not believe him, but dragged my feet with sweat pouring down from my face, but allowed him to carry my small case as I no longer had the strength but refused to part with my backpack.

Twenty minutes later, a repugnant stench tortured my nostrils. We were approaching Madras railway station. I felt that we were approaching a sewer rather than a station.

"Nice smell, no!" laughed Max

Throughout our walks, Max had been attempting to coax information from me, but hit a concrete wall every time. I was not interested in him or his life and I had no intention of becoming buddies with him.

"Cattle class is cheapest. But I think you might find that too difficult. For me it is free", he added with a wink.

I did not think that I wanted 'cattle class' either. I had seen photos of people hanging out of windows, doors and even sitting on top of the carriages.

So a first class ticket was purchased for me and a platform ticket was purchased for Max, with my money.

The platform was chaotic with vendors selling food and drinks from baskets on their heads. The luggage that people carried came in the oddest shapes and sizes. It should have looked a bright, happy place with the brilliance of the colours that were worn, but instead it looked poor and bedraggled with too many flies and men with dirty sarongs. The stench was not quite so bad inside the station, or maybe I had just got accustomed to it.

We did not have to wait too long for the train and Max settled me into a carriage with my bags and told me he would find me at every stop. I assumed he was going to be hanging out of a cattle class window, but felt safe that he was going to be on the train and even safer hugging my backpack with the new knife and the dagger on my belt.

The first class carriage was very mediocre with mostly middle aged men in badly fitting suits, smoking cigarettes and reading newspapers. They would occasionally shoot a glance in my direction, curious about my appearance and my nonchalant demeanour. I stretched my feet across the opposite seat, rebellious and ill mannered, daring anyone to remark or make a request to sit opposite or next to me. I perceived all these fatherly figures as males who dominated their wives and daughters and was grateful that somehow I had been blessed with an existence with freedom to do as I please. However, the hurdles I had to overcome had been a painful struggle and I had been moulded into a person whom I sometimes did not like.

I longed to close my eyes and rest, I was so tired, hot and hungry. How Max remained looking cool and cheerful was beyond me. I had wanted to buy food off the vendors but I was anxious in case I got food poisoning or diarrhoea. I had eaten well on the flight and resolved to last until I reached Indira's place. I had no idea what to expect other than a poor shack in a little village.

They probably had no food even to give me a meal. I realised the value of having Max tag along, he was free spirited and appeared to have no commitments. How he survived or where he lived was a mystery. His name itself was odd, Max was not a typical Indian name, either he had made it up or he was from a Christian family. Religion was something I had no interest in. The little black statue that I carried around with my mother's ashes, its only significance was that my mother treasured it.

The lush greenery swept past as the noisy train trundled through the countryside. The air that rushed in through the open windows was no longer dusty but fresh and moist. The temperature was still high and my clothes stuck to my body, I longed to peel them off and step inside a cool bath, knowing full well that would not happen.

I must have finally drifted into a deep sleep as I was woken by Max shaking my shoulders, "We're nearly there, wake up!"

We finally arrived at Kurnool over four hours later. I had slept through many stops and many of the other passengers had already disembarked at the earlier stations. Max sat undaunted in the first class carriage with his platform ticket.

Momentarily, I was disorientated, forgetting where I was and looked blankly at Max, who said cheekily, "I have been sitting here for ages. You were sleeping with your mouth wide open and snoring".

I came back to reality and annoyed that Max should be so graphic and tactless.

He laughed, "It's good you had a good sleep. We have to catch a bus next. But I am very hungry."

I sighed as if annoyed but was eager to eat a good plate of rice and curry too as hunger and thirst was now needed more than a bath.

CHAPTER 16

The station was practically deserted except for a handful of passengers and the ticket collector.

"I will see you outside the station" whispered Max and disappeared through the connecting doors.

The ticket collector examined my ticket and my attire thoroughly without blinking even once. He questioned me in Tamil but it was too fast for me to understand.

"Pardon? Can you speak slowly please"?

"Alone? Yes?"

"No, my cousin is coming to meet me".

He looked around and saw Max trotting towards us from behind a bus, grinning.

The Ticket collector appeared to scold Max before letting us both get on our way.

"He was shouting at me for not being here on time to meet you. He doesn't know that you are a tough cookie with a knife!"

I handed Max my bag and slapped him on his back good naturedly, "How did you magic yourself behind a bus?"

"Everyone tells me I am slippery! But you have nothing to worry about! Let us find somewhere to eat now".

Max amused me and feeling refreshed after my sleep, I followed him into the village centre.

"This hotel will be okay!"

"Hotel! It's just a greasy café!"

"The food is good here and cheap".

The 'hotel' owner looked at me suspiciously as we slid into the plastic chairs nearest the door. There were other tables with only men, it seemed that women did not venture into 'hotels' alone or accompanied. Everything looked grey and dirty, if my mother had been alive she would have scrubbed the place into a shining parlour.

Max ordered chicken biryani for us, which was served on cracked plates and no cutlery was offered. With our fingers we scooped the aromatic and delicious meal and stuffed our hungry bellies while the other customers eyed me and my bags. A bowl of water was placed on the table to wash our hands and we had to shake them dry. Armed with bottles of water, we left and made our way back towards the bus stop.

Max had no idea when the next bus would come.

"Who knows, maybe today, maybe tomorrow!"

"This is madness, Max, we can't just wait here hoping a bus will come one day, some day!"

"There is a timetable, but nobody knows it. I don't think the bus driver knows it either!" he laughed.

I sighed, shrugging my shoulders, exasperated with his idiocy, envious of his free, untainted spirit. I was desperate for a bath, I smelt of sweat, my hair was matted and greasy and now my fingers smelt of the spicy biryani.

We sat on the mound, Max calm and patient, myself, angry and frustrated. Three men, wearing sarongs, pitched between their waist and knees approached us, muttering quietly between them.

"I am getting a little worried" whispered Max.

I unzipped the front compartment of my rucksack and firmly held the dagger in readiness.

The three men stood around us, "Bag! Give your bag!"

Max bravely tried to remonstrate in a pleading tone but was punched back immediately by the nearest assailant. He fell back into the long, dry shrubs, stunned by the impact, yelping in pain.

The three men circled me, tugging at my clothes and my bag, while I held on tight with my right hand firmly on my dagger and my left hand brandishing the knife. They sneered and swore at me, taunting in the same way Abha had taunted my mother. I had no fear and was ready to rise to the ugly encounter. I gently pulled out the blade and stood square to face them. I lunged forward and plunged it deep into the thigh of the nearest man, drew it out and plunged it in and out again rapidly. He screamed in agony, the other two men were momentarily paralysed but even before they got closer to me, I had my dagger at the face of the next man and was ready to thrust it into any part of his body, be his neck or his eyes, such was my anger and venom.

They backed away in horror, dragging their crying friend, shouting at me "shaytan! shaytan!"

I would have run after them and finished the job if it hadn't been for Max calling out, "Enough! Enough! Let them go!"

Max had scrambled up to his knees and peered at the men through the bleeding cut over his eye and pressing his shirt against his bleeding lip, "You are too quick! I hope the bus comes before the police!"

I stood with my heart racing, adrenalin oozing through my being, buzzing with the success of my defence. I was growing keener to display my talents to Abha, to show him what a coward he truly was.

I poured a bottle of water over my knife washing it thoroughly, gave it a little kiss and placed it back safely in my bag.

"Max, I see a bus. Is that a bus?"

"Praise be to all the gods!!"

"Wipe your face quickly we need to get moving!"

We clambered on the bus, sitting at the very back, packed with the men and their chickens and bags with all kinds of clanging, aluminium ware.

CHAPTER 17

The whole trip so far felt as if I had travelled back in time a hundred years. This was where my mother had started out in a pitiful life of servitude and abuse. I imagined that like myself she had been unwanted and unloved by her father. I recalled our little outhouse, always sitting on the floor in the corner of the gloomy kitchen. I was sure that her life and home before her marriage was much poorer and dreary.

The evening was now drawing to a close as we walked along the dirt track, Max with his constant chatter, excited that we had almost arrived at our destination.

The village seemed to be nothing more than a few rows of houses, all small bungalows, with dusty pastel walls and shuttered windows. The unkempt gardens were splattered with a few clay pots growing bright flowers. Looking for an address was impossible without asking someone. It was apparent that the only way was to mention names as all the inhabitants appeared to know each other. Max used his easy friendly charm, chatting to people as if he had known them all his life. They in turn warmed to him, but eyed me with curiosity and suspicion.

"Your auntie's house is down this track. I have brought you safely!" exclaimed Max increasingly excited as if this was his adventure.

I did not mention that it was I who had practically saved his life. I was nervous and excited, momentarily wishing I was wearing something more traditional, without the blue hair or my tattoo.

I wanted to know about my mother and see her home. The last thing I wanted was to be driven away by Indira or other family members. This would be the first time I would be seeing my grandparents, if they were still alive. I felt a trite embarrassed by my appearance.

"I don't want to go to the house yet", I said to Max, "I need to sleep and wash. I need to feel and look better than this!"

"Oh dear! There is no Hilton here, tough cookie!"

"Don't call me that! But we have to rest and wash somewhere!"

"Under the stars and a nice river bath in the morning! Good?"

"River? What river?"

"Krishna! We have to keep walking past their house, down and down the hill!"

I felt uplifted hearing the word 'Krishna', "River Krishna! Yes! Yes! Perfect! Let's go! Hurry, it's getting dark!"

I knew instinctively that this was the very route that my mother had used all those years ago to carry water back to her home. She had occasionally given me glimpses of her previous life, where she had romanticised the chore, swayed with an urn on her head, splashed her sisters with water, hid among the reeds by the river just for a peaceful moment.

As we approached the glistening calm water, I could feel my mother's presence thick in the air around me. I could smell the fragrant coconut oil that had smoothed her hair into its elegant braid. Whenever she spoke of the river Krishna, I could almost feel the waters as she wrapped her arms around herself as if to bathe and become as one with the river. This was the place to scatter her ashes, but not the time.

Max and I made ourselves as comfortable as we could, laying our heads on mossed mounds and fell into an easy sleep with exhaustion from the stress and heat of the journey.

"Thanks, Max, for staying with me. I couldn't have got here alone."

Max was already asleep, like a happy child, carefree and unencumbered by the burdens of life.

Early next morning, Max was sitting at the river bank, throwing stones.

"Did you sleep well?"

"I always sleep like a baby. But you are a big snorer and your mouth was open again!"

His bluntness was something I was now used to, "How deep is the river? Can I easily have a wash in there?"

"Oh yes, no problem! But take your knife or the crocodiles will get you", he grinned.

"Go and sit further up and make sure nobody comes near us until I finish bathing. I just can't wait to get in there. What about you?"

"I have finished my bath. You want to smell me?"

"No thanks!"

As Max walked away to find a suitable vantage point for a look out, I quickly undressed and waded into the edge of the river in my underwear, armed with soap and a flannel. The morning water was freezing and I could feel my body shuddering with the cold. As my body got accustomed to the temperature, my body swayed while my arms gently floated on the surface. The current was gentle and kind to my body and my feet touched the smooth pebbles as I tiptoed. I dipped my head under and scrubbed myself. It was invigorating and I would have happily lain there with the waters flowing over my head. I imagined my mother with her beautiful long, black hair shimmering in the morning sun.

"It won't be long, mum. You'll soon be free."

I got dressed, putting on the longest and baggiest T shirt I had and a little make up.

"Ok, Max, let's see what today brings."

"You look clean, but your hair is still blue!"

"So what! Let's go!"

We approached Indira's house, there were no closed doors, no doorbells and no knockers.

I tapped on the open door.

"Hello! Is anyone home?"

A middle aged woman peeped from behind a curtain opening into the back room.

"I'm looking for Indira".

The woman rushed forward, covering her head with her shawl as she approached, "Karishma?"

"Yes, it's me!"

She grasped me with her yellow stained hands, hugged me, drawing me close. She wailed in Tamil, stopping to wipe her eyes and face and then hugging me once again. She stroked my blue hair shaking her head, not quite understanding its significance.

I patted her shoulder as if to reassure her that I was quite normal.

From the corner of the dim room croaked a voice, "Yare? Yare?"

An old, wrinkled man sat in what appeared to be a child's chair, he was squinting trying to focus on my form. He snorted, pinching powder from his rusted snuff box, sneezing and wiping his nose with a dirty handkerchief.

Max took over and asked several questions from Indira, both speaking in quick fire Tamil.

"This is your grandfather. He wants to know who you are. Your auntie says that he is practically blind. Your grandmother is in bed; she is also very ill."

Max was very sombre, feeling sorrow for their predicament and offered to go back into town and get food and provisions for them. I handed over a small roll of notes to get whatever would be appropriate. I was not totally heartless although they had thrown my mother out.

I sat with my grandfather while Indira prepared tea and offered biscuits from a tin, which appeared to have a few ants who had taken first pickings. I drank the tea and declined the biscuits. I was feeling very hungry, hoping that Max would get back as soon as possible.

Indira spoke in limited English and I had an understanding of limited Tamil. But somehow we managed to communicate, sitting in the childlike chairs in the dim room.

I told her that I had her sister's ashes and wanted to scatter them in the river Krishna and also wanted to trace my father. She was unmoved by any of this and simply nodded. I asked her about my mother's childhood, marriage and her life in general. Every sentence increased Indira's vehement defence of the care they took of my mother. I knew how unkind her parents had been to my mother and how they all had thrown her out when she had been raped. But Indira's conversation was a pack of lies and I felt my anger and hatred against my father and my grandfather rising to a piercing scream in my head. I wanted to vent the hate I felt at what my mother had undergone, but clenched my fists and stayed in control and listened without showing any other emotion.

My grandfather too listened quietly, I could see that tears pricked his eyes, or maybe it was the snuff, but I felt no compassion for him. They had all colluded in her suffering and now they were all suffering, deservedly.

I sat with my grandmother for a while, she lay on a mattress, the sheets dirty and as I stooped she held my hand with a tight grip, again sobbing to erase the memory of her cruelty. I felt no pity for their predicament. Indira stated that Devi had told them that my mother had ruined Abha's life and killed his son. He had returned to India in despair and was now remarried, running a successful business and had two sons. She assured me that she did not believe all the rumours and knew that my mother had always been docile in her demeanour and had the patience of a goddess.

She told me the name of his export business in Madras and was sure that Max would be able to find it. She also wrote down the address of both his new family home and that of Devi's.

Max finally arrived with a sack full of all the staple groceries, chicken and vegetables. Indira set to work with Max and I, helping her to cook a much longed for meal. The process of having to clean the rice of stones and wash everything thoroughly, took much longer. But the meal was delicious, even if the chicken was probably an old hen with dry toughened meat.

Indira boiled some of the chicken separately and made broth for her parents, the nourishing meal perked everyone up.

I told Indira I was going to scatter my mother's ashes in the river. She saw us to the door and gave me flowers from a clay pot but did not express the need to come with me to the river. I gave her a quick hug knowing that I would not stay in touch, their struggle was their own. However, I did press a few notes into her hand, it was not much, but even if it helped to buy medication for the elderly parents, it was better than nothing. She closed her palm around the notes, nodding her head in thanks and backed away into her gloomy home.

CHAPTER 18

It was still early in the evening, but Max and I decided to camp by the river and set off back to Madras the following morning. We had packed some rotis and chicken for our meal and Max cheekily produced some cans of Indian beer from his pockets.

"We can have a party tonight! I'll make a fire!"

"Is that safe? I don't want to set the whole jungle alight!"

"This is not the jungle! This is our beautiful Mother Earth; she will take care of us".

I smiled and watched as Max started to clear an area. I gathered dry twigs while he dug a small pit using his hands and rocks.

I wanted to scatter my mother's ashes before the sun went down and asked Max to stay with me. I did not want to be alone.

We sat on the river bank and between us was the black urn, the black statue with its gay, red ribbon and the flowers from Indira.

I wanted to say a prayer but could find no words that would fit the moment. I did not think that God had done any favours for her during her short tragic lifetime. All I wanted for her, was peace and release from her pain. I needed forgiveness for my ignorance of not being able to protect her, being a child was no excuse.

I sat there muttering away all my thoughts, getting more and more agitated in my grief. Tears were streaming down my quivering face. I finally stood up and waded into the water, knee high, opened the urn and let the ashes caress the river as it flowed past. The cool breeze made me shudder and the scent of the coconut from my mother's hair lingered in my nostrils. I saw her beautiful smile as she faded away, but knowing that she would never truly leave me. Her presence would be with me forever. I gently dropped the urn into the water, followed by her precious little goddess which winked at me as it bobbed along the river. Max floated the red flowers which followed the statue, like a funeral procession they all floated away.

I felt strangely at peace. All the guilt in me seemed to have floated down the river along with the ashes. Max and I scrambled back up on to the bank. I was grateful for his presence. A total stranger, but like a little brother my mother had sent to be with me when I said goodbye.

Max lit the fire, the sun had gone down. It was pitch black except for the glow from the flames. We leant against each other, back to back, drinking beer and confessing our exaggerated guilty secrets and sins. We plotted and planned on how to escape the curse of revenge and resurrect a forgiving lost soul, but we both always held back, skimming through the present and the future, never the past. The flames flickered and we dozed into a blissful abyss.

The next morning, I awoke to a whole new world where my burden felt lighter but still the mission of finding Abha had not faded. I was not willing to let go.

"So what will you do when you find your father? Will you live in India and stay with him?"

"I actually came to kill him!"

"What! Kill your father!" he screamed, "You want to die in jail! Indian jail is worse than cattle class on the train!"

"I sometimes want to kill all men! All they seem to want to do is to control, hurt and dominate women! It disgusts me!"

"Come on, tough cookie! Let's go kill your father!" he joked to make light of my unpleasant words.

He lifted my bag onto his shoulder and marched in front of me, it seemed that he had had enough of my company and wanted to be rid of me. We bought masala dosais for breakfast and ate on the bus, which once again was busy with merchants off to the town to sell their wares. We arrived at Kurnool, and this time I insisted on buying two first class tickets as I feared the eagle eyed station master. The last thing I wanted was to arrive back at Madras alone. Despite the noisy chugging and clanging of the undercarriage, we both had a pleasant nap, I, resting my head on his bony shoulder.

Travelling seemed to go on for an eternity in India, where at the end of every journey I would feel sweaty and dirty. We arrived at Madras in the evening and Max took me to a small hotel, where the proud owner showed us to a whitewashed room with two single beds and an adjoining bathroom as if it was the Savoy.

The beds were low with lumpy mattresses and pillows but looked reasonably clean. The bathroom consisted of a sunken toilet and a pipe for the shower, only cold water. There was a ceiling fan in the bedroom but the owner said that there were frequent power cuts so unlikely that they would work.

We took it in turns to shower and freshen up, then Max went out to bring back some food for dinner. He warned me to lock the door from the inside and not to open it to anyone until he got back.

I was getting anxious that after over two hours, Max had still not returned. I sat on the bed with all the articles spread out which Joan had given, reading and re-reading each item. I had given the addresses which Indira had written to Max to look up so that we could head over first thing in the morning. I had my dagger on the bed in case of intruders, but no longer eager to thrust it into another living being. I thought of my mother, I was not living the life that she had suffered for. She had wanted me to be educated and live wisely. I felt despondent, torn by my now diminished desire to thrust my anger upon Abha and the longing to let go and move on. But I had to face him and demand that he acknowledged the pain he caused and at least know that he felt some remorse and if the consequence was that he died, then so be it. He had rejected and abandoned me. I was not going to let him off lightly.

Max arrived on cue, excitedly, with packets of biryani, beer and all the information and contacts for our mission for the next day. We fought the flies and ate our meal before falling into a restless sleep on our bug filled mattresses.

Life started early in Madras then seemed to fade away after midday when the sun burned down. Max had already sneaked out and brought back some buns and tea for breakfast.

My return flight was in three days and my money was disappearing fast.

"Your father is a rich man. He is exporting tea to England and other places!"

"No, we have to go and see my grandmother first, I've given you all the addresses. She may not want to see me, but I'll try anyway."

"We take tuktuk. I have found the right man; he will take us everywhere. But we buy him lunch and give little money."

"That's great! I couldn't bear to walk anymore!"

Although we had booked the room for a further two nights, Max insisted that we left no personal belongings in the room.

The tuktuk driver was a small, thin man with a grey cloth wrapped round his head, turban style. A small nod to me and eye contact only with Max, he seemed to prolong the discussion about the best route to take to the first address. Fortunately, Max barked instructions at him to ensure he did not take 'the short cut' to increase his final fare. However, I did not mind that everyone seemed to want to grab money, they only needed it to survive and there was no shame in that.

We arrived at my grandmother's home, which looked neglected and dusty. I remembered it having pale pink walls and pots with bright flowers on the veranda, which my mother tended.

Now the cracked clay pots lay lightly filled with dry earth and twigs adding to the neglect and unkempt, ghostly vision. I walked round to the side where I remembered the barn type kitchen door used to be, where the old ladies would pop in for tea and gossip. The top half was open and I cautiously approached the door, my heart hoping that I would be remembered and welcomed.

Max walked protectively behind, but without hindering me.

"Maami!" I called out as I looked into the kitchen. I was frightened of being turned away, especially now understanding from Indira the rumours that had surrounded my mother.

A shrivelled old man sat on Devi's chair. He was rocking himself, mumbling, not hearing or seeing me. A young, ragged girl came in through the back door, the door that led to the outhouse where my mother and I had lived.

"Enna? Yare?" called out the old man.

Max took over and questioned the girl who was watching me fearfully.

"I'm sorry, she says that your grandmother died last year after a heart attack. That is your grandfather. He is very sick, this girl and her husband look after him in return for a place to stay. The sons don't visit very often since their mother died."

I had no interest in approaching my grandfather, "ask her if I can take a look out the back?"

After a short conversation we were led through the back door to the cemented backyard. The outhouse stood as before but no longer had a curtain draped across it. Inside was dark as I expected but smaller than I remembered. It now looked more like a place you would house your dog rather than a mother and baby. Tears pricked my eyes, how could anyone keep a member of their family, a mother and baby in an unprotected shed like this. I recalled the day when Anil had dragged my mother by the hair to this hell hole and shuddered with disgust.

I looked at Max, "This was where my mother and I lived".

Max nodded sympathetically. If it was not for the fact that my grandfather was a sick old man, I would have beat him and spat abuse at him for what he did to my mother. I came back into the kitchen and looked at him hating the very sight of him. I wanted to shake him and remind him of what he did but it would be useless.

"Let's go" I said abruptly to Max, who silently followed me back to the tuktuk.

I was saving my venom for Abha. He would have to pay for his sins as well as those of his father and mother. They had kept us in a shed like dogs, while my mother had cooked and cleaned for the whole family.

Max calmed me and asked if we could just stop somewhere and have some tea and he had a friend that he would like me to meet.

"What friend! I'm not here for a social visit. I want to go straight to Abha's stupid office," I screamed which was named after my dead brother, Adnan Enterprises.

"I'm frightened for you. I don't want you to kill anyone. There are other ways to make him pay. Please let's go and see my friend. He will advise us. I trust him. He is a very good man".

"Another man!" I sniffed in contempt, "you may think he's good but there are not many good men around!"

"Yes, yes, I know you think that all men are bad, but my father used to say that men are like mangoes, sometimes sweet, sometimes sour and occasionally very rotten."

CHAPTER 19

"I am not going inside this police station! Whatever for?"

"Please, you promised to see my friend. He works here, let us talk to him. Or I can ask him to meet us at the teashop or somewhere."

I did want any control to be taken out of my hands. I had no trust or inclination to believe that the police were going to do anything about Abha.

"Ah Inspector! Long-time no see!" called a delighted Max to an aging, overweight policeman as he stepped outside the building.

"Max! How are you, son? I was looking for you only yesterday!"

"We were just coming to see you and ask for your advice".

"Well ok, then, but I have only a few spare minutes. Come! Come! Let's go back in".

After much protestations I followed, sulking at having been railroaded into accepting the offer.

"So tell me, Max! What have you been up to? And where are you from, your English is excellent."

"Well, Inspector, Karishma wants to find her father. It seems he is wanted for a crime in the UK".

I put my head in my hands and shook it in despair. When Max spoke with such innocence, it strangled my mission and made me feel childish.

"Now take all the newspaper cuttings and show the Inspector. We must tell him everything."

I took a deep breath, getting increasingly cross with Max.

The Inspector spoke softly, "It's okay, please relax. I know Max would not have brought you to me unless he knew there was a very good reason and a chance that I could help".

So it happened, that beginning with a stutter and a stammer, he gently wheedled out of me the past, the present and the projected future of vengeance but not my murderous intentions. Max listened transfixed and I occasionally sobbed, but collected my composure each time to finish my story. I had never unburdened myself so wholly and completely and had to keep going back each time I remembered something I had omitted before.

The Inspector examined the newspaper cuttings, police statements, Abha's photograph, the death certificate and autopsy report for my mother. He took down the details of the import, export company and asked us to come back the following day in the afternoon.

I had no expectations but felt some inexplicable confidence in the Inspector. There was also a sense of relief to unburden myself and that it seemed that there was someone with legal power who may be on my side. But it was not going to prevent the confrontation that I had planned.

Outside the police station, I confided in Max, "I still want to go and see the house where they live. I want to see his wife and children. I'm just curious."

Max looked at me dubiously, "No trouble! Okay! We just hang around outside the house! Promise?"

"I promise!" I assured him.

"If you mess up, you will spoil the Inspector's investigation".

"I said I promise! They are my half-brothers; I just want to see what they're like".

"Come on let's go!"

We found the tuktuk man sitting on the dirty pavement, eating bread and fanning himself with his dirty handkerchief. I felt guilty that he had been waiting for us in the heat for over two hours, while we had been in a cool office drinking tea.

"Don't worry!" said Max, "He is a happy man because he has a job!"

So we once again clambered into the Tuktuk with my suitcase and bag and headed off to find Abha's home address.

The house had brilliant white walls that glistened in the sunshine. A gardener was outside sweeping the path from the iron gates to the house. On either side of the path were carefully landscaped bushes and blossoms. I felt a twinge of envy and a rising anger that Abha should be rewarded in life with such a luxurious existence when all he had shown to my mother was brutal hatred.

Max sensed my mood darkening and gently held me back by my arm, looking at me and shaking his head.

"Let's just go inside, I'll tell them we're lost. I just want to see them!"

"Not a good idea!"

"I'm going in on my own, you can hide somewhere with the tuktuk man!"

"You should not go in alone, not with your knife!"

"Don't be silly! I'm not going to kill anyone; I have no quarrel with his new family. I just want to see! Go now! Go!"

Max reluctantly left me, taking my suitcase, and disappeared round the corner with the tuktuk.

I approached the main door with my backpack and my money belt. I looked like a lost tourist.

The gardener nodded to me as I approached. I just waved to him and pointed to the door and he turned away assuming I was just another visitor.

One of the double doors was slightly ajar and I knocked on it as I called out, "Hello! Is anyone home?"

I stepped into the marbled hallway and a slightly plump, pretty woman glided in with her silken sari from an adjoining room.

She looked at me shocked and started talking very fast in Tamil.

"I'm so sorry to startle you!" I said in politely, "and I'm afraid I don't speak or understand Tamil very well."

"I'm on holiday here and I've just been wandering around and seem to be lost", I continued.

I smiled sweetly and courteously.

She studied me and smiled back, "Where do you want to go?" she asked in an odd fake accent.

"Just back into the main city centre. You have a beautiful garden and house. I've been to some really awful places. Could I trouble you for a glass of water, please?"

After hesitating awhile, she nodded, "wait here, please" and disappeared into the back of the house where I could hear young boys shouting, while the woman called out for a glass of water.

The hall had framed photographs of Abha with his wife, another with both the sons and in pride of place was a large framed photograph of his mother, my grandmother with a floral garland draped over the frame. She looked just as I remembered her as a child. I looked on with sadness that I had not managed to see her again, although I knew that she too had been complicit in the ill treatment of my mother. But there had been a kinder side to her and I felt sure that if she had known the truth she would have saved us somehow.

The woman returned with a glass of water and two young adolescent boys lingered behind her, curious of their strange guest.

"My sons", she introduced, "they go to English schools."

"Hello!" I said to them smiling, "I hope you enjoy the language!"

"Yes, we like it", said the older one smiling, "we are going to England on holiday soon."

They spoke with the same sweet accent as Max with a strange lilt to their intonation.

"Well make sure you take an umbrella! It always rains in London!" I laughed.

They seemed a sweet family which made me feel even angrier as if I had been robbed. Their world would soon collapse if the Inspector did his job and if he did not, then I would ensure that Abha paid the price.

I sipped my water slowly, not really wanting to leave. My conflicted mind desperately wanted to hurt and destroy this family as punishment to Abha and as a homage to my mother who should have had this privilege.

An engine purred to a gentle halt outside.

"It's daddy! Daddy has come home early!" the boys rushed past me and out to the drive to welcome my father.

His wife too, lifted her hand up gracefully, signalling me to wait as she glided to the open door, smiling contentedly.

Abha was going to get a big shock.

CHAPTER 20

The family of four, arms linked, happy faces all jaunted in, laughing and chattering. I barely recognised him, his face glowing with happiness and pride. I hated him more than ever.

Abha saw me and froze. He knew my face; I was the image of my mother.

"It's okay darling, she's a lost tourist from London!" assured his wife.

"Get out! Get out of my house!" growled Abha.

His wife and sons were taken aback in shock.

I stood my ground, resolved to hurt and mutilate his cosy home.

"Hello, father!" I coolly replied, "Aren't you going to introduce me to my brothers?"

The whole family now stared at Abha and me.

"What is she talking about, daddy? Who is she?"

"All of you, go to your rooms! Now!" he gently pushed the boys up the stairs and they scampered off, but lingered on the landing. His wife brushed his arm away and stood her ground.

"She is your daughter? You have a daughter?" she questioned with a tremor in her voice.

"No! She is not my daughter! She and her evil mother killed my son!"

"Son? What son?" his wife was getting increasingly agitated, "Get back to your rooms!" she yelled at the boys who were cautiously descending towards the drama. They were spellbound by the revelations.

Abha stepped towards me, hand raised ready to slap and push me out of the door. I flung the glass of water at the family portrait screaming, "You haven't told your sweet new family how you killed my mother! How you treated her like a slave! How you raped her!"

The boys ran back upstairs and slammed their doors, unable to listen to any more. His wife was even more hysterical, "What is she talking about? Abha! Abha! Who is she? Tell me the truth!"

"She is a disgusting liar! Look at her! Just look at the state of her! Are you after money like your mother?"

"My mother did everything for you and suffered for it! You treated us like dirt and then you killed her!"

"She killed my son, she did not even know how to take care of a child! She was an ignorant woman from the village. I took pity on her to give her a better life, what do you know! You were just a child; it was lucky that my mother brought you up or you would have been dead too!"

I hated the garbage he was expounding and knew the words which would be worse than a knife through his heart.

"You raped my mother and I was born. Your father raped my mother and my brother was born!"

Abha was aghast, his fury unleashed, his eyes bulging and red "You filthy devil with a filthy mind! Get out of my house! You're not my daughter! Get out! Get out before I kill you as well!"

His words registered with me and his wife, it was like an admission of guilt.

"Yes Adnan was your brother not your son," I smirked, "Like father like son!"

His wife had left the hall and was holding her head and knocking it against the door frame, listening to all the ugly words and accusations.

Abha punched me in the stomach and I flew against the wall, hitting his mother's portrait. The garland over the frame slipped off and landed in a heap by their ornate table. I picked a vase and smashed it onto their polished marble floor. He lunged at me again and slapped me so hard, I fell back banging my head against the table corner.

His wife screamed and pulled Abha back, "Stop! Stop! Please don't hit her! What is the matter with you! She is just a child!"

Abha was panting heavily in an ugly rage, the distorted version of his previous life where he had been the victim no longer rang true.

"Is this what you did to my mother? Left her with bruises, broken bones and left her to die! I remember all the nasty insults you hurled at her every drunken evening when you came home from work!" I had plenty to say to him, I had not finished yet.

"I took her to England! I could have left her to be stoned to death by her father! I should have! I did more than enough for her!"

"I know servants and stray dogs who were treated better! You are an evil man! You are a rapist and a murderer!"

"Your mother was a prostitute! She was a whore! You know nothing!"

"You killed her! You are wanted for murder in the UK! I will make sure you go to jail and pay!"

His wife stared at Abha, terrified by these words and backed away.

"Please, my darling Prahbi, don't listen to her. Haven't I always been a good husband to you? We have a good happy life with our sons. She has come to destroy us with all these lies! She just wants money! I know what these people are like!"

Pratibha turned and ran off not knowing what to believe. Her world had been shattered. I smirked as I looked at Abha's splintered expression.

He looked at me in disdain, saliva leaking out of his snarling lips, "So what do you want!?" he sniggered, "money like your mother, a better life? Yes?"

"I want you to admit to murder for a start! And then how about rape! I want you to understand how much you made her suffer. You treated her like vermin and then you killed her!" I shouted, getting up and holding the back of my head in pain. My hand was covered in blood and I felt a trickle down my neck and I still did not reach for my knife.

"I don't know what you're talking about! It is money you're after, I know! All my money was spent looking after the both of you. She used me to get out of her pathetic village! You can't blackmail and threaten me!"

I could not believe my ears that he was in so much denial and that he really believed he was my mother's saviour and she had been wily enough to capture him.

I was desperate to puncture his heart and see him bleed. But for now it was enough to destroy his life and make him pay, death would have been less painful. I took pleasure in seeing his high morals thrown into the gutter and watch his family torn apart.

Max walked in taking in the scene, "Are you alright?" he asked looking anxiously at my bloodied hands.

I nodded, "Meet my father, the man who killed my mother and abandoned me!"

"I see!" spat Abha, "You have an accomplice to rob me. I know the police chief very well, he will put both of you behind bars for a very long time! You won't blackmail me!"

Max studied Abha, "Yes, that's a good idea. I think we should call the police straight away."

"You little scoundrels! Get out of my house! Get out now!" Abha barged forward shoving us both out of the door causing us to tumble down the steps onto the drive.

"It's not over yet, dad!" I yelled putting the stress on the 'dad', as Max and I got up off the tarmac fairly satisfied with unsettling his pampered life. I could not resist taking out my blade and plunging it repeatedly into the tyres of his car and scratching the paintwork while Max tried to drag me away. I picked up a stone and threw it at the windscreen as a parting shot.

Abha shouted back, "you're just a petty criminal and vandal. You have no class just like your common mother. The police will be after you soon!"

I was used to his unkind words, many an evening in our flat in World's End I had heard them over and over again. It was always about our lowly class and my mother's uneducated village upbringing. He would call her a prostitute and an ugly fool that no one would ever want.

I merely shrugged my shoulders knowing that the last thing he would do would be to call the police.

"I should have come sooner!" said Max looking worried.

"I told you not to come at all! But I'm glad you did or I probably would have killed him"

"That would have been a very bad idea!"

"I don't think my mother would have been happy, that's the only reason, or would have liked to tear his nasty heart out!"

We got into the tuktuk and went back into the city, relieved that I had been able to finally confront Abha and vent my frustration.

CHAPTER 21

We went back to the hotel to freshen up before going out to find some food. I wished I could have placed a spy camera in the Abha household to see what was going on. I wanted him to be rejected by his wife and robbed of his sons. He did not deserve the existence that he had created for himself.

Madras had a different feel at night compared to the day. It was still hot and muggy but there was a calmer and cleaner feel to the air. We walked along the streets with Max giving me details of his various missions and errands he had performed for the locals and some businesses. He acted like everyone's eyes and ears and exchanged bits of information to make his way in the world. His survival instincts were strong and could smell trouble from unsavoury tourists and would disappear quickly before they smothered him.

The next morning, I should have both been overjoyed, but sadness was creeping in as the day and time of my departure loomed ahead.

After breakfast we made our way back to the police station where the Inspector was waiting for us frowning.

"Good day, children", He smiled benignly, "It looks like everything is coming together and we may be able to make the arrest and then get him extradited. But not all can be done in one day!"

"I don't trust all the paperwork! He'll find a way to pay someone off, he told me himself!"

"No dear, not when we have international orders and not when it's murder!"

It seemed like strong evidence that Abha would be arrested once the final authority had been given by the chief of police and the embassies on both sides of the oceans had finalised the process. I was still not fully convinced. I was disappointed that I would not see him handcuffed and dragged away from his opulent marble floors and see him begging for mercy from behind bars. But having ripped apart the family and destroyed his peace was satisfaction enough for now.

"Thanks, for your help. I probably won't see you again as I fly tomorrow and it's unlikely that I will come back, there's no reason."

"You never know child, you might come back under happier circumstances, a holiday or maybe to find out more about your half-brothers".

"I doubt that, but goodbye anyway!"

He rose from his chair and we shook hands. He then looked at Max over his spectacles,

"Come back here tomorrow after your friend has gone. We have a lot of work to do!" he winked and shook Max's hand.

Max nodded and backed away following me onto the dusty road to our waiting tuktuk.

"I'm going back to the house!"

Max looked at me annoyed, "What is the matter with you! Why can't you leave it now?"

"I want to know what's happening in their house," I replied.

"Your choice! I'm not coming. I'm finished! You can take the tuktuk and pay him off".

"Well, thanks for your help. How much do I owe you?"

But Max was already walking away as if I was diseased with an unsatisfied revenge. I felt judged and it made me angry,

"Well fuck off then! I hope nobody rapes, beats and murders your mother!"

He never looked back and putting his fingers to his ears disappeared into the crowds.

The tuktuk driver looked at me warily, I smiled not wanting to frighten him away also. He took me back to Abha's house and I directed him to wait out of sight, I showed him some banknotes as his reward. Poor as I was, in India I felt like a millionaire.

I left my suitcase in the tuktuk as all it now contained was dirty laundry and a few spare t-shirts. My back pack had all my documents, clean shirt and underpants for the next day and my dagger. My sheathed knife was in my back pocket, always ready for an attack.

I had no plan or reason for returning other than to gloat at the broken home.

I looked remarkably wilder than the day I had first arrived in India. My hair had grown with the black now showing at the roots and the blue considerably lightened by the sun. It had become wiry and frizzy with the humidity and sweat and was too short to tie back. My skin was even darker with sunken eyes because of the lack of sleep and stressful days. My tattoo was never intended for beauty, but now had a sense of evil. My bedraggled clothes looked poorer than those of the street urchins. It was surprising that max had not deserted me some time ago.

But here I was outside the grand gates of my father's home once again.

I slinked around the trees and shrubs on the inside of the gates, trying to gauge any activity within. It was quiet. There was no gardener in the grounds. There were no cars on the drive. I hid my back pack by a tree, holding on to only my dagger and knife. The front door and windows all appeared to be firmly shut. I weaved myself through the garden to get a closer look, still lurking in the bushes and out of sight. There were no shadows or signs of movement. There were no sounds of children's chatter or the bustle of family life.

Had I managed to destroy Abha's life so easily, or was this just a temporary lull in the storm. I could not trust that when I flew back home tomorrow, things would remain irreversible. I wanted concrete evidence that Abha's life was destroyed.

I walked around to the back of the house, still keeping my distance, my eyes sharp and my ears straining for sound. I moved in closer and a breeze brought forth the familiar stench of beer and cigarettes. Abha was at home, probably alone. I could feel my heart beat faster and my chest heaved as it groaned with the adrenalin rushing into my brain. My hands gripped tightly on to the dagger and my knife pressed reassuringly against my thigh in my jeans pocket.

I crept silently forward like a panther who had found its game. Abha was sitting at the side of the house, laid back in a deck chair with his back to me. Empty beer bottles and whisky bottles were strewn around, curls of smoke reached up from his chair. Intoxicated flies buzzed around angrily. Abha's hand reached out with a rolled newspaper to beat them away, but they only returned to torment him. I walked out to the side in a wide curve, aiming to move in front of him, still keeping my distance and still keeping my eyes fixed upon his drunken body. He caught sight of me and the ugliness of his gaze poured out the hatred he had towards me.

I now stood directly in front of him but about ten feet away, returning his gaze with equal hate and venom. He looked at my dagger and I noticed a slight flinch in his eyes before he regained control. I sensed fear entwined in the anger. I had no fear and stood strong, my courage came from within and not from my weapons. I could have lunged forward easily and taken out his heart and his last breath in that second but that would have been too easy for him. I still had not seen him suffer. I wanted to see him beg for his life and to beg for forgiveness.

I took slow steps towards him, he drew in a long gasp from his cigarette and let the smoke curl out from the corner of his lips. He then swigged back gulps from his whisky bottle to prove his indifference to my presence. I was nothing to him. I was of no significance. As yet, not a word was spoken by either of us.

I was now barely two feet away from him and reached out with my dagger to gently caress his throat with the blade. I knew his body had tensed up but chose to take another swig from his bottle, looking at me straight in the eye. The buzzing flies and mosquitos wanted blood and crisscrossed before us excitedly. I brandished the small blade from my pocket and slashed the side of his face and he gasped inwardly in pain, but still remained slouched in his deck chair and took a deep suck from his cigarette. Blood dripped down from the gash onto his white vest while the flies buzzed about fighting in clusters to join in the feast.

I could not leave him like this. I had to finish the job. Abha was shaking, although the whiskey had desensitized his pain, the fear was apparent. He was like vermin caught in a trap and there would be no escape or compassion.

I threw down my knife and lifted up the dagger with both my hands and held it above his chest. He sat frozen, beer in one hand and a cigarette in the other. His blood shot eyes in disbelief that I was capable of plunging the dagger into his breathing mortal soul. If only he would utter even one word of sorrow or regret, I would have walked away. Nobody chooses in life to kill their father.

We looked into each other's hearts for five long seconds and found nothing to cherish. There was no remorse. I thrust the dagger with all my strength, deep into his body only moving my head back as the blood spurted out. He convulsed for an eternity with blood coming out of every orifice until he finally lay, a limp corpse with eyes wide open in horror and shock.

I pulled the dagger out smoothly and threw it on the ground next to the knife. I took the garden hose and turned it on to wash down the weapons as I hated to see blood sodden knives. I no longer had any need of them and left them beside the body. I walked away to my back pack and changed my T-shirt wrapping up the blood stained clothes in old newspaper.

Back at the tuktuk, I gave the man the rest of my rupees and asked him to take me to the airport promising him a little sterling when we arrived. On the way, I threw out my bundle of clothes down one of many gutters of garbage and pestilence.

The journey was over; I was going back. I had no family, no home and no money but I had a sense of closure to enable me to move forward and start a new life.

THE END

Printed in Poland
by Amazon Fulfillment
Poland Sp. z o.o., Wrocław